**A Border Agent
Mystery**

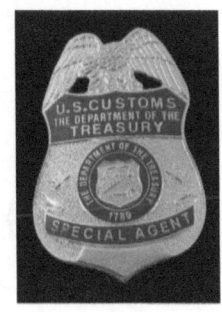

Illustration by Matt Butcher

Border Lake

Ray Summers

Wynona Press

Wynona Press
wynonapress@gmail.com
www.borderagentmysteries.com

This book is dedicated to
Janet Wynona Cloninger Summers,
my high school sweetheart and loving wife of 62 years.

Thanks to artist and illustrator
Matt Butcher
for enhancing the Border Agent Mystery series
with his work.

A very special thanks to
Retired Customs Agent Office Assistant
Frances Luna
for her insight and edit of my first
cobbled-together version of "Border Lake."

Prologue

This mystery novel is set in a time period from 1960 to 1973 before the advent of the Drug Enforcement Administration, a time when U.S. Customs Special Agents freely roamed both sides of the of the U.S./Mexico border from Brownsville, Texas to San Diego, California investigating and enforcing laws, overseen by the Treasury Department. I was one of those agents during those years.

Some incidents and most of the locations in this story are based on personal experience and observations. The beautiful "Border Lake," Amistad, is real, as are the numerous sites of native pre-Columbian pictograph and petroglyph art mentioned in the book. However, there are no gambling casinos in Mexico near Lake Amistad, and gold has never been found in the area.

The story in this mystery novel "Border Lake" is fiction. It never happened, but during this time period it certainly was possible.

– *William R. Summers*
Retired Senior Special Customs Agent

Map by Matt Butcher

Ray Summers

1

Offered unlimited use of a Boston Whaler in return for its repair and refurbishing, Sarah Dobbs politely refused, explaining that a sailboat would not meet her needs. The owner of the Whaler laughed and said, "Come take a look."

Sarah took a look and ever since had been looking at and from the sixteen-foot, eighty-five horsepower outboard motorboat. She and the Whaler became almost inseparable prowling the waters of Lake Amistad above what had mainly been the path of the Rio Grande between the United States and Mexico.

As a landlubber from the New Mexico desert, she knew little about boats. When she heard "Whaler," Sarah thought of old sailing ships such as the Pequod in "Moby-Dick." Now, two months later, she was much better acquainted with boats and boating.

As she steered the motorboat one afternoon toward a large sailboat anchored near the end of a now-very-familiar secluded cove, Sarah was thinking that this would be only her second contact for the day. Fall school registrations had begun, turning this great body of water that was teeming with boats over the summer into a ghost lake.

Earlier, miles to the south, off the point of a cigar-shaped landmass jutting from Mexico known as *La Bolsa*, "The Pocket," she had intercepted two sport fishermen. They turned out to be locals, men she had spoken with before.

She had given them business cards with her New Mexico address and telephone number of the shop she owned there. "This is my last week," she'd informed them. "I must return home. Please let me know if you see or hear anything that might interest me." She offered them the eight-by-ten flyers with photos and descriptions of Laura and Mike and the scant details of their disappearance on Lake Amistad. They also had her local phone number. The fishermen said they still had flyers from her last visit. Sarah apologized for the interruption and eased the Whaler quietly away.

The bright-orange flyers in English and Spanish were everywhere now, on both sides of the border, at the marinas, campgrounds, motels, laundromats, grocery stores, fast-food establishments and gas stations – wherever she had been allowed to post them. A facsimile of the flyer had run in both local newspapers: the Del Rio, Texas, *News-Herald* and the *Zocolo* in Ciudad Acuña, Coahuila, Mexico. If anyone in the area was unaware that Sarah Dobbs's sister and brother-in-law had gone missing on the border lake it was no fault of Sarah's.

She could make out three bikini-clad figures on the deck of the tall-masted sailboat ahead. She had never seen a sailboat this far north of the dam. And anchored in a narrow cove? It seemed strange. Sailboats belonged on Lake Amistad's open water, not in the confines of a Rio Grande side canyon.

Thoughts of the sailboat vanished as prickly rays from the low afternoon sun crept under the wide brim of her straw hat. The tender flesh of her peeling nose could take no more punishment. She lowered her head slightly, returning full shade to her face. The dry, speckled hands gripping the steering wheel came under her scrutiny. Hard to believe they were hers; it was distressful to Sarah to know that her face exhibited the same sun-ravaged condition. Hat and sunscreen had failed her miserably. The tan cuffs of her long-sleeve shirt reminded her that the thin, billowing cotton had not failed. Beneath the flowing fabric, her soft, fair skin still survived in dazzling contrast to mottled body parts left exposed. This small victory brought a painful smile to Sarah's cracked, dry lips. Retrieving a tube of lip balm from a shirt pocket, she removed the lid and gently stroked the waxy balm onto her tender lips. Replacing the cap, she noted that a mere stub of hazy ointment remained. She dropped the tube back into her pocket. This one she would not have to replace.

Two college students had kept her gift shop in Socorro, New Mexico, The Spotted Pony, going all summer. They would be returning to campus a week from tomorrow. She would soon be a shopkeeper again... if a tax matter with the IRS could be worked out.

Shopkeeper. That seemed alien now, somehow not at all appealing. As her departure date loomed, Sarah began to realize that she was no longer the same person who had arrived on the Mexican border two months ago. What would people in Socorro think of the new Sarah? Would anyone even recognize her? She glared at the ragged nubs on her hands that had once been pampered with routine professional care. The nails had been the first to go. Two excruciating encounters with bow and anchor lines had been enough. Then the hair. She had tried to save her hair. Braids at first, then a ponytail. But there was no time for the care of long auburn waves. What now remained slid easily into the crown of a warped, wide-brim straw hat.

She smiled, remembering how offended she felt the first time she was mistaken for a man. Not such a bad thing, she quickly realized, not when prowling Lake Amistad's wild uninhabited backwaters alone. At the same time Sarah also thought that, at a distance, any attractive thirty-five-year-old woman in jeans and turned-down cowboy hat could easily be mistaken for a man. A dried-up, skinny old man now, she thought. She could have spared ten pounds, but weeks of dawn-to-dusk exposure in the open boat had melted away twenty-five pounds. Agile and strong, mean and lean – Sarah liked her new self.

Fifty yards from the anchored sailboat, she realized she had made a mistake about the bikinis. The three women on deck were naked. This quick assessment was confirmed when two nude men appeared beside the women, stared in her direction and retreated to the boat's cabin. The women remained on deck, waving excitedly to her. *Wrong, darlings*, Sarah thought, *I'm not a man*. The name "La Luna Azul" glistened in tropical pink from the sailboat's stern. Without slowing, Sarah put the Whaler into a wide left turn. She would visit with the people on The Blue Moon another time... when they were dressed.

She maneuvered the boat steadily along the winding mile-long inlet toward the main channel, her sharpened eyes now instinctively searching the widening shorelines on either side. Laura's cap had been found in this cove off the Rio Grande arm of the lake, thirty-six miles north of the official search area. Border Patrol agents on routine lake patrol delivered the faded red cap bearing The Spotted Pony's logo to park rangers two weeks after the disappearances. Laura and Mike had each taken a cap from the gift shop last summer – Laura a red one, Mike a blue one.

Park Rangers had performed only a cursory inspection of the cove, refusing to expand the official search area, maintaining that the swamped boat could not possibly have drifted such a distance. Theories that the cap belonged to someone else or that Laura had lost it prior to the accident were offered. Sarah had no theory regarding Laura's cap being found so far away from the boat. She knew only that the Devil's River arm of the lake had been thoroughly searched and that the Rio Grande arm had not. Her heated discussions with Park Rangers were the first indications that after two weeks of fruitless searching, official interest in her sister and brother-in-law had begun to wane.

A ride aboard the Border Patrol boat to the location of the cap's discovery was the last assistance she received from U.S. federal authorities. Credibility there was long gone.

Clearing the cove, Sarah shoved the throttle forward and turned north up the Rio Grande toward the national-park boat ramp twelve miles away. The eighty-five-horse Johnson outboard was not overly loud, even running near full throttle, but the long late-afternoon runs to the boat ramp left her ears buzzing if she didn't protect them. Shaking soft silicone earplugs from a plastic vial, she rolled them into balls and pushed one into the opening of each ear... and failed to hear the distant rumble of rifle fire echo from the cove behind her.

♦   ♦   ♦

Eleven-year-old Mario Ortega-Mendoza heard the shots. He dropped the armload of dry limbs he had gathered for his evening fire and hurried toward the cove. The shots sounded like those of the deer poachers who sometimes cruised the lake at night with powerful spotlights. But it was too early for them. It must be the Border Patrol. They often shot the rough *carpa* fish with their *pistolas* when no one was around. The patrolmen always had something for him: fruit, cookies or a candy bar. Mario gave two sharp whistles, informing Nacho, his cur sheepdog, to take charge of the goat herd. The border patrolmen would pay money for three large flint arrowheads he had unearthed yesterday.

At the cliff's edge, Mario's excitement faded. Only a sailboat. A glance down the cove in the direction of the main channel of the Rio Grande told him there was no Border Patrol boat, no fruit, no candy and no money. He glanced back at the large sailboat below. Something was going on. Three naked women were face-down on the deck. A man with no shirt stared at them as he fastened his trousers. The sound of another shot caused Mario to flinch and take a step backward. The man on the sailboat dropped to his knees and fell across the women. The shot had come from the south side of the cove, but movement on the north side caused Mario to turn in that direction.

A small, dark-haired young man wearing a bright-blue shirt was clawing his way up a steep hillside a few yards north of the cliff. Another shot stopped his frantic scramble. Mario flinched again, taking another step backward. The man in the blue shirt slid slowly back down the incline, his shirt gathering under his arms. Mario had seen this man before, yesterday, a mile to the south, wearing the same blue shirt, paddling a red canoe. Mario had sat watching the man in the canoe for a long time. The double-bladed paddle seemed to move the canoe effortlessly and gracefully across the smooth water. Mario had thought how wonderful it would be to have such a canoe and paddles. The blue shirt covered the man's face by the time he slid from sight behind a small bluff.

Mario turned in the direction from which the shots had been fired. To his right, above the cliffs surrounding the cove, a graveled slope merged with an expanse of dense blue-green cenizo brush. Mario knew this mesa. It stretched southward some two kilometers, ending at other cliffs surrounding another cove. Whoever fired the shots was hidden by the dense cover, perhaps even now aiming the rifle in his direction.

This thought hit Mario like the bullet he suddenly expected. He spun away from the cliffs and bolted for the nearby mesquites. He had planned to move the goats northward in the morning, allowing them to graze the lake shoreline for another two days, arriving back at his family's fishing camp the day after tomorrow. But the goats could just as easily move westward, away from the lake, at least for a day. He whistled softly to get Nacho's attention, gave him the hand signal for silence, then the signal to gather the herd for moving. Mario gathered his few belongings and hurried to help Nacho. As he stumbled over the firewood he had gathered, another shot rolled up from the cove. He decided then that there was no need for a fire tonight.

2

"He told me to take off my clothes," sixteen-year-old Jill Cowden said. Customs Special Agent Ryan Shaw stared at her across the table. They had been over this before. It was easier for her this time, but not for her parents. At the far end of the long dining table in their San Antonio, Jack and Louise Cowden sat stiffly in high-backed chairs. Jack Cowden inhaled, folded his arms and continued to stare at his daughter. Ryan glanced down at his cassette tape recorder on the table in front of the girl. A red light indicated it was recording. "All right, Jill, the inspector told you to take your clothes off. Go on from there, please."

"I told him no – that I wasn't going to do that. That's when he held up the bottle of pills. It was a small, clear bottle containing 20 or 25 yellow-and-black capsules."

Her description of the pills was perfect this time, plenty of detail, and Ryan needed detail. It would be an experienced customs inspector's word against a teenager's. He would edit out his own questions and comments from the first transcript of the tape. The revised pages would become the girl's sworn statement of what had happened to her last Friday evening at the U.S Port of Entry at Amistad Dam, just north of Del Rio, Texas.

A nervous Jill continued, "He said he found the pills in the car and that we could be sent to prison for five years. I told him they weren't ours. He said the pills were found in our car and that was all he needed to arrest us and confiscate the car. I asked him to please not do that. He said he wouldn't if one bottle was all we had." Jill took a deep breath and glanced at her parents. "He said he had to be sure."

Jill and her older brother Ted had left early Friday morning on a mission for their father. They had driven from their home in San Antonio to the border town of Del Rio to deliver a briefcase he'd forgotten. They were then to head directly home after lunch, but Jill had suggested a short drive north of town for a look at Lake Amistad. Ted had remembered hearing of a hotel and gambling casino that had recently opened on the Mexican side of the lake. He tried to take responsibility for the excursion into Mexico, but Jill claimed the drive across the dam into Mexico was her idea. She said they had lost all track of time after meeting a group of young people from Austin at the new casino. Neither disputed the fact that by early evening, Ted was drunk. Someone had helped Jill put him into the back seat of the car. A short time after dark, Jill drove them back across the dam to the U.S. port of entry.

"He said he would let you go if the one bottle of pills was all you had," Ryan prompted.

The girl turned to face him, eyes welling up. "They weren't our pills." Her voice broke and tears streamed down her cheeks. "I had never seen them before, and I knew they weren't Ted's. Someone must have dropped them when they helped me put Ted into the car." She began to sob. Mrs. Cowden offered her granddaughter a handkerchief.

Jill's sobbing subsided. Mrs. Cowden returned to her chair. Ryan leaned forward. "Just start with what the inspector said after he showed you the pills."

As Jill took a moment to dry her tears, Ryan recalled how just yesterday in Washington, D.C. he and the new commissioner of Customs had spent what was left of Saturday evening in the Capitol Hill office of U.S. Senator John Merewether Cowden. The senator from Arizona was livid that his granddaughter had been strip-searched and fondled by a United States Customs inspector.

"He said, 'Take your clothes off,'" Jill recounted, "'Show me that you're not carrying anything else and you can be on your way.' That's exactly what he said."

Ryan nodded. She had remembered to quote the customs inspector.

Jill took a deep breath and continued. "I didn't want to call Daddy or home and upset everyone. I thought we could get out of it without anyone knowing. So I did what he said. I took off my shoes, shirt and jeans. Then he said, 'Everything, take everything off.' So, I did. I took off my bra and panties. He said, 'Raise your arms and turn around.' I did. He said, 'Lean against the wall and spread your legs.' When I did that, he came up behind me and put his hands on my breasts. I screamed. He backed away, blocking the door so I couldn't get out. He told me to get dressed. I put my clothes back on, and he moved away from the door. As I left, he held up the bottle of pills and said, 'Five years if I see or hear from either one of you again.'"

Jill finished by saying that she rushed to the car and drove away. She did not know the inspector's name but had described him earlier in the statement. Ryan reached toward the recorder, his hand hesitating midway. "As you removed your clothing, what did you do with it?"

"I put them on a bench that was there in the room."

"Did the inspector examine it, search the pockets?"

"No."

"What about your shoes? Did he look inside your shoes?"

"No."

"And he never searched Ted?"

"No, he tried to wake him, make him get out of the car, but finally gave up and just looked around the back seat." She glanced toward her parents, apparently uncomfortable drawing attention to her brother's condition.

Ryan turned off the recorder. "I think we're done for now," he said quietly.

"What's our next move?" Jack Cowden pushed away from the table and stood. He was 42, a year younger than Ryan, as Shaw recalled, near the same six-foot height with a similarly slender, raw-boned build. Cowden's short blond curls no longer covered the paleness above his ample, flaring ears. His dark blue eyes seemed paler now. Noticing eye color was a lifelong habit for Ryan, his own being of an uncommonly blue-green hue. His contrasting turquoise eyes and cropped, almost animal-fur-thick black curls seldom failed to elicit attention and even stares from the opposite sex.

"Back to the airport, and on to Del Rio for me." Ryan answered as he retrieved the recorder and placed it into his silver metal briefcase and shut its lid. "And to see what Customs Inspector Banner has to say about all this."

Ryan had been furnished all the information that the Commissioner of Customs' staff could assemble on short notice. The accused Customs inspector had quickly been identified as Chuck Banner, a thirty-year-old with less than two years service.

"No flights to Del Rio," Cowden said shaking his head. "No airline serves that area. If it did, I'd be their best customer. Del Rio is a two-and-a-half-hour drive by car from San Antonio, I can tell you that for certain."

Ryan stared thoughtfully at Jack Cowden. Twenty years ago, when he first met him, Jack was manager of the family's large cattle ranch just east of Nogales, Arizona. Since that time, Cowden business interests had expanded to encompass U.S.-owned factory operations in Mexico. Known along the United States/Mexico border as *maquiladoras*, these enterprises were the result of agreements between the U.S. and Mexican governments that allowed for temporary import of material and/or parts from the U.S. for assembly in Mexico and return to the United States as salable merchandise. Jack Cowden had evolved from an Arizona rancher and record-holding rodeo cowboy to the CEO of a very complicated but extremely lucrative Cowden family enterprise.

Ryan broke that train of thought. "Then it's back to the airport for me anyway, rent a car and drive."

Jack insisted on driving him to the airport. As he backed his silver-gray Cadillac from the driveway. he commented, "I sure was surprised last night when Dad called and said it was you that was coming," He glanced in Ryan's direction. "You haven't changed much. Stuck you behind a desk yet?"

Ryan nodded. "They finally wrangled me into an office about three months ago. I managed to stay overseas, Spain mostly, for eight whole years. I'm back in the States now, training Customs agents at the new Federal Law Enforcement Training Center here in D.C."

Jack turned into a freeway on-ramp. "Training, huh?"

"We have a new commissioner," Ryan continued the catch-up conversation. "*She*," he emphasized, "is a former Chicago district attorney. She insists that she is committed to having the best law-enforcement agents in the country. I'm supposed to help crank 'em out for her."

Cowden stared into his side-view mirror, accelerated and slid into a small void of freeway traffic. "A desk for me, too," he said. "I managed our first two factory sites in Nogales and Aqua Prieta from the ranch, but two years ago we expanded to Ciudad Acuña and Piedras Negras. Now I get back to the ranch maybe twice a year." He shook his head as if just realizing something and turned toward Ryan. "If you're running a training camp, what the hell are you doing investigating this incident?"

Ryan smiled. He didn't recall promoting himself to head of the training academy. "The senator," he replied. "It was either me or a congressional-subcommittee investigation. The new lady commissioner couldn't assign me to the matter fast enough."

Jack laughed loudly. "Of course," he said, chuckling. "The senator. Well, by God, it sure as hell pays to have connections."

Ryan smiled. Yes, he thought, and this little girl, Jill, wasn't exactly a slouch in the connections department: a senior United States senator grandfather and the senator's son, *maquiladoras* entrepreneur Jack, for a father.

♦   ♦   ♦

If it weren't for Ryan's connections, he would be at the training center. His recommendation for a decent Spanish course had been approved. Competent instructors now had to be found, equipment leased…. How had he ever gotten himself into this crazy, massive training-overhaul program? Conned? No, even a commissioner couldn't trick him into his near-miserable present situation. No, he had not been conned. Threatened?

His eight-year overseas working vacation was over, the new commissioner of Customs had said, standing over the contents of a personnel folder scattered across a large worktable. Ryan assumed it was his folder. He understood that the commissioner had ordered a large, ornate desk removed from her office, replacing it with three long worktables. Ryan noticed when he entered her office that there was no desk in sight, just tables.

With little explanation, the commissioner informed him of his options. "I'm upgrading all Customs special-agent training," she said. "Experienced agents from every field will be overseeing but not necessarily instructing every phase of a new extensive training program. Your record indicates you worked the Mexican border prior to being assigned to Europe." She paused, glancing at documents before her. "Quite successfully, it would appear. You have three choices, Agent Shaw: The Customs training facility performing whatever duties I decide; assignment as a street agent again wherever the Office of Enforcement chooses to send you; choice number three, I'm sure you have already contemplated."

Optional retirement age for federal law-enforcement officers is fifty. That was seven years away for Ryan. He could accept one of the other choices or resign. The possibility of working the street for supervisors ten years his junior certainly helped make a persuasive case for his involvement in the commissioner's super-agent training scheme.

This unexpected assignment had actually begun to intrigue him. With parental notification of small drug seizures from minors being mandatory, Ryan's first thoughts on the situation had been that the kids were caught with a few pills and made up a wild story to cover themselves. This should take two days at most to confirm. The senator would accept the embarrassing truth from his trustworthy old Arizona border agent, and everyone could go back to work. That's what he had first thought.

♦   ♦   ♦

Ryan stared into the oncoming freeway traffic as Jack drove him to the airport. But it wasn't going down that way. Best he could tell, the kids were telling the truth.

Jack maneuvered to the outside lane and entered the off-ramp.

"The senator never forgot how you busted those cattle rustlers. He brings that up every time we're at the ranch."

"Just luck," Ryan said. "I happened to have people in the right places, that's all."

"Having people in those kinds of places is hard work, not luck," Jack said. "And maybe you could have made a lucky two-hundred-yard shot, but not three. Two Jeep tires, and a leg out from under Camacho Fuentes. Not luck, but damn good shooting." Jack Cowden struck the steering wheel with the heel of his hand and shook his head.

Ryan was silent. Last night the senator had slapped the top of his desk after making the same proclamation, but the senator had been louder, much, much louder. No, the senator had never forgotten, and neither had Ryan. There was much trouble over the shooting of Camacho Fuentes twenty years ago; two internal-affairs investigations, a civil suit haunting witnesses and federal court dockets for almost six years.

The senator was attorney general of Arizona at the time of the shooting. Small numbers of very expensive cattle had begun disappearing from his ranch just east of Nogales. State Attorney General John M. Cowden suspected Mexican rustlers and requested federal assistance. Ryan's sources in Mexico came up with the time and place of a planned raid by local rustlers. A twenty-man federal and state task force, including the senator himself, was waiting for them. Ryan was remembering the rifle he had used that day, an old World War II Garand.

Jack interrupted the thought. "Did you marry that pretty girlfriend of yours, the public-health doctor that worked down at the port of entry? La Rubia, we used to call her."

Ryan sighed. Mary Margaret Casey, nicknamed La Rubia for her vibrant blonde hair, he thought, beautiful, wonderful.... "Nope, I still haven't done the marriage thing yet. That was Mary Casey. She had always wanted a medical-research job, finally got one with the United Nations Health Service. She left Nogales while I was in New York on special detail. That was the fall of 1958."

"I don't think I ever saw her without you, except when she was working down at the port, of course. Everyone thought you two were bound to spring a surprise wedding on us just about anytime."

"I thought so, too, Jack, but it just didn't work out." Something in the tone of Ryan's voice ended that topic of conversation. Jack became occupied with airport-terminal maneuvering. Nothing more was said until he pulled up to the curb at the terminal.

"Those kids had no business going across the border to that damn gambling joint," Jack said. "There's been trouble over those Mexican casinos, demonstrations, threats, even a newspaper bombing. Nobody's been killed yet, but everything's ripe for it. My son and daughter shouldn't have gone over there but, by God, when they got back to the United States they should have been safe." Ryan noticed Jack's fingers tighten on the steering wheel.

"That's right, Jack." Ryan said. "I'll take care of it."

3

Monday morning, the sailboat was gone. Sarah dismissed it from her mind and turned the Boston Whaler toward the cliffs forming the northern border of the cove. Her pale blue eyes skimmed the calm surface of the cove ahead. Even the smallest fragment of debris failed to escape her eagle-eyed scrutiny. It was instinctive now, especially here where Laura's cap had been found.

She swung the boat westward along the strip of rocky beach until it joined the towering cliffs that ended the cove. Tightening her turn, Sarah reversed direction, setting an eastward course paralleling the cliffs on the south side of the cove. Noticing a narrow crack in the limestone wall looming ahead, she veered away from the cliff before she remembered that the bees nesting there were gone. She brought the boat back on course. One day, she had ventured too close to the hives in the crevasse and it prompted a quick, ferocious attack. Long sleeves and her fast boat had allowed her escape with only three stings. She had kept her distance after that. A rising lake level had forced the bees out last week or drowned them. She could muster no sympathy.

The lake she had come to know well had been a stretch of desert bisected by the Rio Grande until six years ago, when construction began on the Amistad Dam. Its purpose was to provide flood control, generate hydroelectric power and both conserve water and funnel it to irrigate agriculture in the area.

The lake was a happy byproduct of the plan, at least if the brimming activity on it over the three previous summer months was any indication. Texans loved their lakes; ironically, all but a few of them had been created like Amistad by damming rivers. As the dam across the Rio Grande rose, so did the lake behind it, finally rising to maximum level at the end of the previous summer to create a just over one-hundred-square-mile aquatic oasis along the border between Mexico and the southern end of Texas.

Lake Amistad had been stocked with a variety of bass alongside catfish, crappie, carp and other fish species, immediately becoming a fishermen's paradise. As its first full summer progressed Sarah saw more and more sport-fishing boats on the lake reeling in its bounty; sailboaters, swimmers and scuba divers drawn by its clear waters also increased until Labor Day weekend. Texans and others were delightedly discovering a new recreational vacation destination.

Now in the first full week of September, the lake that had been buzzing with activity was suddenly almost as barren as the desert it had submerged. Ironically, Sarah, who loved the desert lands of New Mexico where she was born and raised, had now come to just as much treasure this aquatic environment even if her time on the waters of Amistad were coursed with the frustration and sadness of still not knowing what had happened to her sister and brother-in-law.

The lake's name, Amistad, was the Spanish word for friendship. And Sarah also enjoyed the people she'd gotten to know and become friendly with there. But simmering underneath that was the specter of something ominous that grew stronger as her search felt more fruitless.

She cruised along the cove with the Whaler at half throttle as cliffs on either side funneled her back into the main river channel. She turned south. It was an hour's run along the twisting switchback course of the Rio Grande to open water on Amistad. Shoving an earplug into each ear, she pushed the throttle forward and settled down on the cushioned bench.

Limestone walls on either side opened occasionally. Some inlets were hardly more than large notches in the towering tan cliffs. Others, Sarah knew all too well, reached far inland, branching, meandering... miles and miles of shoreline. Now it whizzed by in only seconds; long, hot days of fruitless searching; Mexico on the right, Texas on the left. Ahead was more, much more, to be done.

But time had run out. The two college students who had managed the gift shop all summer would be returning to campus next week. She would have to head home by Friday. Sarah dabbed her eyes with her billowing shirtsleeves. She hadn't expected to leave without Laura. Or at least knowing what had happened to her and her husband... God forbid.

For the next hour, Sarah kept the boat in the center of the meandering river channel that often all but doubled back on itself. She knew every turn, every outcrop and overhang of the thirty miles between the confluence of the Pecos and the Rio Grande and the vast open water of Lake Amistad. As she came out of the last steep bend that had sent her back northward for several miles, a low-flying aircraft caught her attention. Slowly, lazily, it passed overhead and banked westward, following the Rio Grande out of sight. Fifteen minutes later, it was back, following the Mexican shoreline southward.

As the Boston Whaler cleared a long, narrow landmass protruding from the Mexican side and headed southward into open water, a second larger airplane approached along the U.S. shoreline. Sarah knew then that someone else was missing. Customs, Border Patrol and private aircraft had flown similar patterns searching for Laura and Mike. Boat and air searches had covered over 500 miles of shoreline on the Devil's River side of Lake Amistad. The wrong side, Sarah was convinced. She glanced down at the brown briefcase strapped to the base of the steering console. Laura's faded red baseball cap with her gift shop's Spotted Pony logo was inside.

Laura and Mike had each taken a cap last summer. Laura had chosen a red one, Mike a blue one. The red one had turned up on the head of an eleven-year-old Mexican boy who lived in one of the many fishing camps on the Mexican side of the lake. A Border Patrolman had turned the cap over to Park Rangers, explaining that the boy and his father had found it while seining for fish bait.

Laura and Mike's rented boat had been found 35 miles southeast of the cove where the cap was found. Sarah had no explanation for that. There was no indication of foul play. The official theory was that the cap belonged to someone else or had been lost prior to the accident. Sarah recalled her heated discussion with the park supervisor over such a presumption. It was the first indication that after two weeks of searching, official interest in the fate of her sister and brother-in-law had begun to wane. The last assistance she received from U.S. government officials was special permission to be taken on the Border Patrol boat to the location where the cap had been found.

Sarah shifted in her seat and moved the throttle forward. She hoped the missing people turned up soon; otherwise they might never be found, like Laura and Mike. Unacceptable thoughts began to surface in her mind; the new search appeared to be along the Rio Grande. The search would continue longer if no one were found quickly. A real search of the Rio Grande might reveal something of Laura and Mike. Horrible... Sarah thought, *what have I become to think such a thing?*

The lake widened abruptly, allowing more than a mile distance between the two countries. The surface was calm now, as it usually was before the afternoon southerly winds picked up. Moving against Amistad whitecaps made for a bumpy ride, very bumpy. Reason enough, Sarah had decided after her first kidney-shattering ride, to make the daily forty-mile highway drive north every morning to the boat ramp where the Pecos and Rio Grande converged. Searching southward allowed for a less painful return trip, usually traveling with the wind. It also allowed morning and evening inspections of the cove where Laura's cap had been found and for the past month an almost-daily thirty-minute swim session.

Sarah skirted the last six miles of jagged Mexican shoreline leading to the mouth of Caballo Canyon. She would have searched here weeks ago if she'd known about the pictographs. The canyon's overhanging walls reportedly sheltered scores of pre-Columbian painting sites. Mike and Laura spent every summer traveling the Southwest in their Winnebago photographing and cataloging such places for a book they had planned. Sarah learned of the Caballo Canyon rock art only two days ago from the owner of the repair shop who kept the Boston Whaler's old outboard motor running for her.

Shelter and pictograph sites were abundant along the Rio Grande and Pecos river channels. Sarah had begun her search weeks ago north of the confluence of the two rivers, systematically working southward until today. Now she was skipping ahead to examine Caballo Canyon. Her time on Amistad was running out.

Drifting near the mouth of the yawning canyon, motor idling, she watched the search planes work the canyons between her and the dam twelve miles to the southeast. She would like a look in those canyons too, but that was not to be. As she moved the throttle forward and began the turn into the canyon, a distant speck of reflection caught her eye. She straightened her turn and reached across the steering wheel for her binoculars. A red-and-white boat, the new Glastron belonging to Chango, was headed her way. She reversed the turn, moving the Whaler out to open water clear of the canyon entrance, and cut the motor.

Sarah knew the owner of the rapidly approaching boat. Robert Andrews was his given name, a descendent of pioneer Texan and Mexican families. A good listener, she knew that family history well from Chango's detailed telling. He was known to all in the area not by his actual Anglo name but by his Spanish nickname.

Lake Amistad had inundated a substantial portion of the Andrews family ranch holdings in Mexico. Most of what was not claimed by the rising water had been confiscated by the Mexican government for national-park purposes. In return for the flooded and seized property, the Andrews family was granted commercial fishing rights for the Mexican portion of Lake Amistad.

Andrews' family members had never been happy with any part of this arrangement, especially when gambling casinos and opulent estates began to surface on the alleged parkland they had once owned. The sole survivor of this once-powerful, influential cattle dynasty, Robert "Chango" Andrews, was now almost within sight behind the split windshield of his new boat.

Yes, Sarah thought, she had been a good listener to Chango's many tales of woe. She had to admit that Chango had been most accommodating. She had accompanied him on his rounds to the Mexican fishing camps. He introduced her to the fishermen and Mexican officials, and was a great help with the flyers she'd had printed in Spanish and distributed in Ciudad Acuña. They asked anyone who had information to contact her.

Chango never failed to stop and visit, and remained persistent in inviting her out. She had always refused. Chango claimed he was not married. This was perhaps true, but Sarah knew that at least two of the young women who cooked and kept house for him had babies but no husbands.

The red-and-white boat circled and came alongside. Three uniformed men were with Chango. "Good morning," Chango yelled in English. That struck Sarah as strange. Chango always spoke to her in Spanish, forcing her to rely on tidbits of Spanish she remembered from high school and a crash course taken while selling real estate in Albuquerque five years ago.

"Good morning," she returned the greeting in English.

Chango pulled the boats together with a boat hook. "We are looking for a sailboat," he said, tying the boats together. "A big sailboat." Chango was wearing his trademark brushed blue jeans and striped T-shirt. Blue and yellow stripes today. Curly black hair covered his arms and protruded from the neck of the shirt. "A monkey or an ape," Chango had answered when she questioned him about his nickname. He had pulled on the hair on his forearm and laughed. He didn't remind her of a monkey or an ape, but more of handsome Greek fishermen she had seen in an old movie. Perhaps her relationship with Chango might have taken a completely different path under other circumstances... one circumstance being the absence of teenage housekeeper girls with fair-skinned babies.

"You seen any big sailboats today, ma'am?"

Sarah grimaced. This wasn't the Chango she knew. His formality tipped her off to how something was wrong. She looked closer at the three men with him: olive-drab uniforms, all in their late thirties, gold-rimmed aviator shades, garrison hats matching the dull shirts and trousers, brown boots, belts, holsters with large semi-automatic pistols. Mexican uniforms all looked the same to her. Gold badges on each shirt indicated they probably weren't military, although three silver bars gleamed from the epaulets of the smallest man. Immigration? Customs? Police? She had no idea. Whoever they were, they had caused a dramatic change in Chango.

"No, no sailboats today." She played the game, searching Chango's eyes for guidance. He looked away. She was about to mention the sailboat she had seen yesterday when the small man with silver bars ordered Chango to cut the engine.

"What were you doing there?" He nodded toward Caballo Canyon. Sarah looked at Chango. Hadn't he informed them about Laura and Mike? Chango folded his arms and stared at his new deck carpeting.

"I have permission from the federal judicial police to look for my sister and brother-in-law," she replied calmly, turning back to her inquisitor. "They disappeared here, somewhere on the lake, two months ago."

"And you thought you would find them in the canyon?

"I wasn't in the canyon. I was going in, but...."

"What did you bring back from Mexico?" Without waiting for an answer the man with silver bars on his shoulders stepped aboard the Whaler.

"Nothing. I have nothing from Mexico. I haven't been to Mexico."

The officer leaned over and unfastened the bungee cord holding the briefcase to the steering console.

"Those are maps of the lake, circulars and things about my sister and brother-in-law." She reached for the briefcase.

The officer pushed her away and glared. The look was chilling; left eye bulging, mouth twisted into a strychnine smile. Sarah retreated a step. "As I said, I have permission." Her voice trailed away into a whine. She hated sounding that way, but this man frightened her. She now realized that Chango was frightened also.

Born and raised in New Mexico, she had heard and read reports of cruelty and corruption by Mexican officials all her life. She was now well south of the Rio Grande channel markers, therefore in Mexico, within the jurisdiction and at the mercy of these three officers. She eased farther backward and sat down on the padded bench seat, eyes fixed on the grotesque face. Slowly, the bulging eye receded, the twisted mouth straightened and the face became almost normal. Sarah could now discern a slight depression on the left side of the man's face. A crushed cheekbone? Automobile accident? Perhaps. Judging from his present demeanor, a boot heel was the more likely possibility.

The man with the sunken cheek slammed the briefcase onto the console, opened it and withdrew a small zippered pistol case. He held it up for the others to see before turning toward Sarah. "A map?" he asked sarcastically. He closed the briefcase, placed the vinyl case on top and unzipped it. His eyes widened, seemingly aglow. The crooked smile broadened as he ceremoniously removed Sarah's small black Browning . 380 semi-automatic pistol from its case. Holding the short pistol grip between thumb and forefinger he turned to display it for the others. "It is illegal to bring arms into Mexico," he proclaimed as he turned back to Sarah.

Sarah was silent, considering what she might say that would not get her into more trouble. A glance toward Chango elicited no assistance or clue. "I can help look for the sailboat," she offered, sounding more desperate than she intended. "I know the lake. I know the lake," she repeated. "I have this boat, gasoline...." She gestured around the boat. "I could help you."

The official ignored her, opened the briefcase again and rummaged through it. He passed her largest map of the lake over to the men in Chango's boat. "The sailboat we are looking for belongs to the mayor, the mayor of Ciudad Acuña." He slammed the briefcase closed and turned toward her. "The mayor and four other people were on the sailboat when it left the marina Saturday morning. It is a very big boat and has the name La Luna Azul."

Sarah took a deep breath. She could take them to the cove. Maybe that would help.

"If you see this boat," the official continued, "or anything suspicious, report it immediately to the marina." The man signaled Chango to untie the boats and stepped back into Chango's boat with the others.

"What about my pistol?" Sarah asked. "You took my pistol."

Chango was at last looking at her, grimacing and shaking his head.

"If you had a *pistola*," said the ugly man wearing the silver bars, "I would have to place you under arrest and take your boat." The eye bulged. His mouth twisted. She couldn't tell if he was angry or attempting a smile. Chango's outboard motor gurgled to life and the red and white boat pulled away, trailing a wisp of white exhaust.

Sarah stared after them. Motionless, eyes welling up. What had she expected? Help? Sympathy? Not exactly, but she certainly hadn't expected to be robbed. Tears streamed down both sunburned cheeks. Dirty bastard! He wasn't going to get away with this. She untied a bandana from the steering console, dried her eyes and looked toward Caballo Canyon. And he wasn't going to keep her from looking for Laura and Mike, either. Sarah pushed the outboard's starter button.

Ray Summers

4

Customs Special Agent Ryan Shaw thanked the loud woman on the other end of the line, hung up the telephone and tossed the thin Del Rio phone directory toward the motel-room nightstand. Reaching across to the other bed, he retrieved the large map of Lake Amistad he had been studying since breakfast. Amistad was a large, dark-blue inverted horseshoe. Its jagged, sprawling shoreline had immediately reminded him of some Asian mural that depicted fighting dragons. The Rio Grande dragon's tail snaked upward toward the northwest, the Devil's River dragon tail northeast. Flooded canyons and washes were claws, feet and legs. Bodies and heads were one elongated mass above the thin white dash representing the international dam.

There was his real interest: the dam and the small red dot near its center indicating the U.S. port of entry. A male uniformed United States Customs inspector had strip-searched a sixteen-year-old girl there. If she had been just any average teenage girl a complaint may have eventually brought a Customs internal-affairs agent out of Houston to investigate. After a review of the internal-affairs agent's report by that department's supervisors, it would have been forwarded to the Customs regional director, who would have appointed a reviewing officer. Within thirty days, a recommendation for or against disciplinary action would have been made. If punishment were recommended, appeal and hearing rights would kick in. Employee union representatives and attorneys pretty well called the shots after that. Final resolution could drag out for months, sometimes years.

But not this time. Justice would be swift for the senator's granddaughter. One shred of evidence to corroborate Jill Cowden's story and Chuck Banner could kiss his shiny gold Customs badge goodbye.

Ryan folded the dragons, slid them into his silver aluminum briefcase and grimaced. Sometimes a shred of evidence could be hard to come by.

♦   ♦   ♦

"Found it just fine," Ryan said to the plump middle-aged secretary who had given him directions on the telephone. Bert Henderson, the Del Rio Customs resident agent in charge, had quickly introduced himself, then disappeared to take a telephone call.

"It's a little confusing since they put the new road in." Jean Harris was as loud in person as she had been on the telephone. "Before, you could just follow the loop road." She gestured toward two lanes of pavement outside the picture window. "It would bring you right here. Well... it still does, but now, with the new traffic light and turnoff south of the school, and all the signs...."

"Damn it." Henderson's voice boomed from the next room. He burst into the reception area. "We'll have to use your car. Mine's down the street being serviced." He stepped around Ryan and threw open a hallway door. "Look out the window," he shouted to no one in particular. "Watch for a light-blue Ford leaving the port." He disappeared through the doorway. Ryan could hear the rattle of metal cabinet doors coming through the open doorway.

Jean Harris moved to the large picture window facing the loop road and peered between the blinds. "He's leaving now, going straight north," she shouted.

Henderson stormed back into the hall, headed straight for the front door, walkie-talkie radio in one hand, green binoculars case in the other, brown briefcase under his left arm. "We'll have to use your car," he repeated and nodded toward the front door. Ryan moved out ahead of him, opening the office door, unlocking and opening the passenger door of his rented white Dodge.

"Damn it!" Henderson was shouting, "I changed that lookout to *hold and call, damn it*! *Hold and call*! I was going to handle this at the port. Always someone who doesn't get the damn word." By the time Ryan moved to the other side of the car, unlocked, opened his door and slid under the wheel, Henderson had tossed his briefcase into the back seat and was working the brick-size walkie-talkie. "Alpha 801 to Alpha 802."

Ryan started the engine, backed out and headed the Dodge northward on the four-lane blacktop that Jean Harris had referred to as "the new road."

"Alpha 801 to Alpha 802 or 804." Henderson slammed the walkie-talkie onto the seat, clawed open the green plastic case and removed a large pair of binoculars. "We're after a powder-blue Ford, 1968, Texas plates, no passengers, driver only." He put the glasses to his eyes. "Don't see it. Must be in front of the traffic." He traded the glasses for the walkie-talkie. "My car is back there," he motioned with his head, "at the Texaco station, and both my agents are out at the lake," Henderson explained. "They may be able to give us a hand if they're not already in the boat." He raised the radio to his face again. "Alpha 801 to 802 or 804."

Ryan moved into the left lane and spotted the Ford three-hundred yards ahead. "He's just rounding the curve ahead." Ryan pressed the accelerator. The Dodge Dart shot past a pickup and two cars and rounded the only curve on the two-mile stretch of State Highway 277 that linked the City of Del Rio to its international bridge.

Brake lights glowed as the blue Ford neared a flashing amber light marking a school zone. Ryan had gained all the ground he wanted and backed off. Fifty yards and two other vehicles remained between him and the Ford. "What's he got?" Ryan asked.

"Don't know," Henderson answered. He gave the small radio a sour look and lowered it to his lap. "I have a city detective in Odessa that calls now and then when he gets word someone is coming down to pick something up." He glanced at Ryan. "Odessa is four-and-a-half hours northwest of here." Henderson turned his attention back to the suspect car. Ryan nodded, recalling a time when informants and contacts had fueled his own excitement.

"This guy has done state time for dealing grass," Henderson continued. "I put him into Mexico Saturday night. Intended to let him run when he came back." Henderson glanced again at Ryan. "You know, in case he took delivery on this side. I changed the lookout when Tom and Gordon had to go to the lake." He raised the radio. "Alpha 801 to any Del Rio unit."

Ryan stared at the Ford ahead, remembering when he used to let them run, weave and circle, check for heat, then pop them when they lined out for home.

The walkie-talkie in Henderson's hand crackled, "This is Alpha 802." Henderson had finally raised someone.

"Tom, the Ford from Odessa got past the port. I'm behind it in a rent car with a visitor. Can you give us a hand?"

Silence, static, then, hardly audible, "You're breaking up... understand you need help. We'll head back to the dock."

"They're already on the lake." Henderson had the radio next to his ear. "Surprised I got them at all." He moved the radio back to his face. "Disregard... disregard. We'll handle it." No response. The resident agent in charge (a.k.a. RAC) lowered the radio and shook his head. "We need a repeater out there. I've pushed for one since I got here." He turned his attention to the suspect car. "Stay with him. There's four ways out of town. When he commits to one, I'll have Jean make some calls and get some help."

Ryan trailed the Ford through the old section of Del Rio, north over the railroad overpass and along a six-lane strip of roadway lined with motels and fast-food establishments. "Avenue F," Henderson identified it. "Also State Highways 90, 277 and 377." Traffic was heavy for the small town, red-light signals frequent. Ryan reduced the buffer zone between suspect and pursuers to just one vehicle. They ambled northward two miles before traffic began to thin. Ryan allowed the Ford more distance. A few hundred yards past the Ramada Inn where he was staying and a sprawling shopping mall, open brushland began to appear. A mile past the city-limits sign, the Ford veered left at a fork in the highway. Henderson raised the small radio and contacted Jean Harris. "Call the Border Patrol. See if they're checking traffic at Comstock today." The secretary acknowledged. Henderson turned to Ryan. "Border Patrol has a checkpoint thirty miles northwest of here. If they're working it today, we'll follow the Ford into it and toss him there." The

RAC leaned back, placing the radio on the seat between them and lifted the binoculars. Ryan turned northwest onto U.S. Highway 90, two hundred yards behind the suspect.

"Move up on him a little," Henderson said. "The road to the dam is a couple of miles ahead, right on a curve. I want to put him past there, then we can back off again."

The Dodge Dart was within seventy-five yards of the blue Ford when it passed the turn-off to the dam. Henderson lowered the binoculars, retrieved the walkie-talkie and placed it on his lap. "I guess you're here because of the strip search."

Ryan nodded. "Know anything about it?"

"Just what I heard from the inspectors. A senator's granddaughter." Henderson shook his head. "I expected IA to come swooping in, maybe even someone from headquarters...." He let the thought trail off.

Ryan finished Henderson's statement, "But not someone from the training staff." He smiled, glanced at Henderson and answered the RAC's next, unasked question. "The girl's grandfather is John Cowden, senator from Arizona, an acquaintance of mine from when I worked the border out of Nogales years ago." Ryan let that soak in a moment. "The senator insisted that I handle this investigation. The commissioner agreed." That was all Henderson needed to know.

"Alpha 800 to Alpha 801," Jean Harris' loud voice erupted from the walkie-talkie. Henderson answered. "Alpha 801, go ahead."

"Border Patrol advises no traffic check today at Comstock and no units available for assist, but a Terrell County Sheriff's unit is between Dryden and Langtry. He's en route to the check station and will stop suspect vehicle for you."

Henderson looked at Ryan. "She's worth two agents, I tell you, maybe three." He hit the walkie-talkie's talk button "Ten-four. Thanks."

"Alpha 802 is ten-eight."

Henderson gave the radio a surprised look and asked for Alpha 802's location.

"Can we go to channel six?" Alpha 802 asked.

"No," Henderson replied. "I'm on a walkie-talkie... no channel six." The RAC glanced at Ryan. "Six is our scrambled channel. It's scanner proof."

"Ten-four," Alpha 802 came back. "Gordon and I are at the high-bridge with... visitors."

"They're ahead of us." Henderson looked surprised again. "I thought they were going to look over the south end of the lake this morning." He spoke into the radio again, "Suspect is north of the lake now, headed toward Comstock. Border Patrol checkpoint is down today, but Terrell County SO unit will be there to make the stop."

"Ten-four, we're headed that way."

Henderson acknowledged with two clicks of the transmission button and leaned back in the seat again. "That's Tom Del Castillo and Gordon Shanks. They're with four ATF agents out of Houston. Tom has a snitch that's going to cross fifty AK-47s for buyers out of Houston. ATF is going to let them run, bust them in Houston and try to keep Tom's snitch cool."

"Fifty AK-47s?" Ryan raised his eyebrows.

"Real ones, confiscated from a Chinese ship by the Mexican Coast Guard in Mazatlán, so the story goes, then... stolen from the armory?" He shrugged and gave Ryan a doubtful look. "Anyway, there are fifty authentic Russian-made assault rifles on a ranch south of Acuña. Tom's man and one of the buyers have already looked them over."

Questions immediately surfaced in Ryan's mind, but he resisted. Informant deliveries were perfectly legal, but defense attorneys seldom agreed. Details of cases like this were best left with those involved. Ryan believed Henderson had already revealed more than necessary.

"There is where the Rio Grande and the Devil's River met before the lake was here." Henderson was pointing out Ryan's window as they started across a long bridge, water on either side as far as the eye could see. Ryan leaned forward and set the trip odometer. Henderson continued, "Now, the lake backs up for over fifty miles up each of the old riverbeds. The dam is back there about a mile south of the juncture."

Ryan nodded. Earlier, he had been impressed with the size of the lake shown on the map. He was again impressed when they reached the end of the bridge. The odometer read two and a half miles.

"Those mountains are in Mexico." Henderson pointed west again, over rolling blue-gray hills of cenizo to a low range of mountains on the horizon.

"How far to the bridge Tom was talking about?" Ryan asked.

"Pecos River bridge is twenty miles north of Comstock... about forty miles from here. There's a public boat ramp there. The Pecos runs into the Rio Grande about a mile south of the bridge. I didn't know they were coming up this way today." Henderson shook his head again. "They're looking for a place to deliver the guns."

Ryan was thinking about the boat ramp being twenty miles north of Comstock and the thirty miles between Comstock and the dam. A lot of border shoreline, and this was only the Rio Grande portion of the lake. Boats from Mexico also had access to the Devil's River arm of the lake. This place was a smuggler's dream.

As Ryan maintained a two-hundred-yard interval between the two cars, the Del Rio resident agent in charge disclosed more details of the ongoing arms-smuggling case, pausing periodically to relay their position to the sheriff's unit ahead. By the time they rounded a curve and saw a revolving red light ahead, Ryan was sure he knew everything about agent Tom Del Castillo's machine-gun case that the RAC did. Another mile and he believed he would have had the name of the informant. Ryan had never been comfortable with such loose talk. He remembered court cases lost, sources compromised, even informants murdered because of it. He would not be sharing anything remotely confidential with Henderson.

The blue Ford stopped next to the brown-and-white Terrell County Sheriff's patrol car. A tall man in a khaki uniform and brown western hat looked on as two men in sports shirts and jeans, pistols drawn, surrounded the Ford. Ryan closed in on the suspect car, blocking any possible retreat. Henderson bailed out, weapon drawn. Ryan stepped out, retrieved his Remington .45 semi-automatic from his briefcase in the car's trunk and joined the others.

A small Mexican man was removed from the car, patted down and handcuffed. Henderson took charge of the suspect. His two Customs agents went to work on the Ford. After a few seconds, the agent searching the back seat called the others over. A compartment under the rear seat cushion held twenty-five baby Mexican yellow-headed parrots. Ryan looked at the frightened little birds and smiled. In the old days, parrot smuggling was near the bottom of an agent's priority list. Comments and looks exchanged between Henderson and his two men told him that parrot case rank hadn't changed, but it was still a violation of federal law. While the agents arrested and questioned the smuggler and made jokes about their catch, Ryan introduced himself to the tall, gray-haired man in khakis.

"Bill Shockley, sheriff of Terrell County," the man responded as he took Ryan's hand.

Ryan explained that he was in the area for only a few days and, like the sheriff, just helping out.

"We stop one for 'em now and then," the sheriff said. "Usually, the check point here gets 'em first." The Terrell County sheriff was returning to his office in Sanderson, 90 miles farther west, from a meeting at the Val Verde County Sheriff's Office in Del Rio. Shockley was pleasant and friendly. He and Ryan discussed mutual friends: customs agents who had worked the Big Bend country west and south of Terrill County. When Ryan noticed the prisoner being escorted to the rented Dodge, he excused himself. When he reached the rent car, the parrot smuggler was in the back seat.

"Agent Ryan Shaw... this is agent Tom Del Castillo." Henderson indicated the stocky mid-thirties agent with thick eyebrows beside him. He shook Ryan's hand with a firm grip. "Over there," Henderson pointed across the car roof to a younger, blond-haired man, "agent Gordon Shanks."

Ryan nodded. Gordon raised a hand and continued walking toward the blue Ford. "Gordon's taking the seized car and parrots back to the office," Henderson explained. "You and I will follow with the prisoner. Tom's going back to his little chore, OK?"

Ryan agreed and sat down in the driver's seat. Henderson walked to the nearby brown sheriff's car. Ryan glanced at his watch. Not quite eleven, noon by the time they got back. A late start, but still time to do something about his own little chore. A talk with Banner's supervisor was number one on the list. Perhaps Jean could call and set up an appointment for him with the Del Rio Customs port director. He leaned back in the seat. This border agent business was untimely but not all together unpleasant since he wasn't doing any paperwork on it. The thought made him smile. He turned to look at the small middle-aged Mexican man seated behind the passenger seat. "What's your name?"

"Ramon Garcia," the little man responded without emotion.

"Have you ever been to Nogales?" Ryan asked in Spanish.

"Never," Garcia answered in English. "I've never been out of Texas."

Ryan shook his head and again spoke Spanish. "We saw you come through the port from Mexico, so you've been out of Texas at least one time."

Garcia was silent. Ryan glanced toward the sheriff's car. Henderson and Shanks were talking and laughing with the sheriff.

"What's so damned funny?" Gracia asked angrily. "Why is everyone laughing?"

Ryan turned back to the rear seat, satisfied that Ramon Garcia was not from Mexico or any place other than the United States. He was a homegrown smuggler. "I think it's your parrots, Ramon," Ryan said in English. "I think they were expecting you to be sitting on a couple of condoms of cocaine, or at least a few pounds of grass."

"Yeah." Herman exhaled and stared out his side window.

The group at the patrol car laughed again. Ryan recalled something another parrot smuggler had told him years ago. "You know Ramon, they'll be laughing in the joint, too, when word gets around."

"I know. Everyone else will be up for dope, robbery or murder. I'll be in for smuggling baby birds." Garcia looked disgusted and stared out the window again.

Ryan faced forward. It wasn't a long wait.

"Can we make some kind of a deal?"

The last time Ryan had been asked that question it came through an INTERPOL Turkish interpreter in South Africa. Ryan's answer to that question had gone back through the interpreter. This time, he didn't need an interpreter to relay the exact same answer. "What have you got to trade?"

"A dealer from Amarillo in an airplane waiting for me."

"Close by?"

"Pretty close."

"What kind of airplane?"

"I don't know, but it's new and has two engines."

"Is he alone?"

"His wife usually comes with him."

Ryan looked toward the sheriff's car. The sheriff and the customs agents were still talking. Here goes the rest of the day Ryan thought as he tapped the horn and motioned for the RAC. Turning again to the back seat he said, "It's not my call, Ramon, but I'm pretty sure you'll be able to cut yourself a pretty damn good deal."

♦   ♦   ♦

Later that day, just after four in the afternoon, Ryan walked across the loop road from the Customs Agents Office to the Del Rio Port of Entry. Herman had made his deal. Preliminary paperwork on the seized plane and three parrot-smuggling defendants would occupy Henderson and Shanks well into the night. Tomorrow the two agents would possibly have, with Jean's able assistance, formal reports ready to mail to the United States attorney in San Antonio. Arrangements had been made to have the plane flown in to San Antonio from an isolated ranch landing strip near Langtry. The $100,000 Piper Twin Comanche now belonged to Uncle Sam. The thought consoled Ryan for a day lost on his own mission.

♦   ♦   ♦

Customs Port Director Sam Griffin was a short, completely bald man with a gnarled face. His office was small. The wall to Ryan's left was a glass partition, revealing a slightly larger waiting room next door where two men stood before a counter as a Customs inspector examined and stamped documents. The wall behind the port director's desk was covered with framed black-and-white photographs of various sizes. Ryan introduced himself.

"You're here about Banner, I suppose." The aged port director shook Ryan's hand, motioned him into a chair and sat down behind his generic gray metal desk.

"Yes, sir." Ryan seldom addressed men as "sir." When he did so it was due to an instinctive feeling of respect for the man being addressed. Weathered old Sam Griffin had instantly struck such a chord in Ryan.

"I'll help you all I can," Griffin said. "Anything I can do, just let me know," Griffin shook his head. "A senator's granddaughter... damn. I wish I could have handled this joker the old-fashioned way. Personnel specialists, union reps, thirty-day notices, hearings, appeals, papers, papers, papers. We just can't get rid of the trash anymore. I would have run his ass off the first time. He wouldn't have been here to take off another little girl's clothes."

Ryan had been studying the enlargements of old snapshots displayed on the wall behind the port director: uniformed armed men posed in front of unpainted buildings, armed men leaning on ancient automobiles, more armed men on horseback and astride thin motorcycles. Ryan's gaze dropped from the photographs and focused on the old man across the desk from him. The Del Rio Customs port director now had Ryan's undivided attention. "There have been others?"

Ray Summers

5

It was dark when Sarah turned off the main highway and drove through the brightly lighted archway of the RV park. She was relieved to be off the road. The lights on the boat trailer were out again. Fortunately, two previous warnings had been from different Highway Patrol officers. The boat and the motor had been refurbished, but years of storage and recent submergences with every boat launching had left the trailer with peeling paint and rotted electrical wires that shorted out often. She would locate and tape up the new electrical short in the morning. She had filled the four gasoline cans earlier after leaving the Mexican marina. A quick wiring repair would have her rig ready for the road and another day on the lake after a little errand to the main Mexican Customs office in Ciudad Acuña.

Sarah waved as she passed the small frame house that was both home and office for the owner of the S&S RV Park. Sally Weaver returned the greeting from her lounge chair on the lighted deck beside the house. The Boston Whaler and trailer belonged to Sally. They had languished in a storage shed for almost ten years after her husband Sam Weaver's death. He had used the boat on the Rio Grande and often trailered it to the coast to fish in the Gulf of Mexico, and would have been delighted by the lake that had now risen nearby.

Sally had offered Sarah use of the boat and trailer when she learned how much Sarah was paying for boat rental. Five hundred twenty dollars for outboard parts, tune-up, lube, fuel cans, trailer tires and adjustments to steering and throttle cables was far less than Sarah had paid for a week's boat rental. Sally had saved her from bankruptcy, then gave her boating lessons and familiarized her with the lake and surrounding area. Sally kept tabs on Sarah, took messages for her if anyone called with tips about her sister and was usually on her front porch every evening until Sarah returned.

At the end of the lighted driveway, Sarah turned right into the darkness. Tall mesquites flowed past her window as she passed two small trailers on the right, a motor home and two vacant spaces before her headlights found the lopsided oleander bush. She made a wide turn to the right and parked. Taking only her hat and briefcase from the Ranchero, she crossed a brittle patch of lawn, inserted a key into the door of a large Winnebago motor home and entered.

The Winnebago that had been Laura and Mike's traveling home every summer was still warm from the afternoon sun. She flipped on the overhead light, closed the door behind her and adjusted the thermostat. The air conditioner kicked in as she dropped the briefcase to the floor and tossed her hat toward the passenger's seat. She kicked her deck shoes off and looked over at her telephone answering machine to see if its red light was blinking to indicate messages for her. The little bulb was dark.

Sarah's shoulders sagged. What was she doing wrong? Someone must know something. But other than getting a few calls when she first passed out flyers that offered questionable leads that went nowhere, her efforts hadn't yielded any answers.

She moved to the rear of the motor home, stripping off her thin, long-sleeve shirt. No progress and the lack of new tips weren't going to get to her tonight. This had turned out to be a good day, the only one she could remember since Laura and Mike disappeared. The thought brought a twinge of guilt. She grimaced, ashamed that her first reaction to the missing sailboat had not been concern for the mayor and his party but that now there would be a massive search of the Rio Grande arm of the lake. A callous thought, but she had topped even that by brazenly arranging to have her own flyers passed out to the Mexican search parties.

Sarah stripped off her blue jeans and collapsed facedown on the double bed. This was when she usually cried. Alone, tired, frustrated and depressed, she sometimes sobbed for hours. But not tonight. Finally, things were looking up... all because that bastard had stolen her pistol.

Sarah rolled over and sat upright, frowning at her mental image of the Mexican officer. What grotesque facial expression would he make when he had to return her pistol? The thought made her smile.

After brooding over the pistol incident all day, she had skipped her usual restaurant stop in Comstock and gone straight to the dam, unhitched the boat and trailer and driven across to the Mexican marina. She had been elated to find that Señor Armando Fuentes, the federal judicial policeman who had given her permission to search the Mexican side of the lake, was coordinating the search for the mayor and his party. Fuentes was genuinely appreciative of her information on the sailboat. He apologized for the way she had been treated and told her she could pick up her pistol from the main Customs office in Ciudad Acuña in the morning. During their conversation, she'd overheard talk of a Coast Guard unit being sent from Matamoros. This would be a thorough search. She had left her entire supply of Spanish-language flyers. Senor Fuentes had graciously promised that they would be passed out.

Sarah unsnapped her bra, trying to imagine gift shop owner Sarah Dobbs being that pushy. The two-month ordeal had certainly changed her. She dropped her bra onto the bed. "You've come a long way, baby," she said and stepped out of her white panties. Callous thoughts and brazen behavior were in order. No one would look for Laura and Mike after she left.

Sarah opened the door to the cubicle that contained both toilet and shower. She was about to step inside when a soft knocking startled her. She stared at the front door, wondering if she had locked it. She never had visitors. Mrs. Weaver sometimes phoned if she hadn't noticed Sarah's arrival, but she had noticed tonight, and she always phoned, never came in person. The soft knock was repeated, like that of a child.

Sarah pulled a terry-cloth robe from the nearby closet and slipped it on. "Who is it?" she shouted, walking toward the door. The windshields of the motor home were sealed with foil inserts. The other windows were covered by heavy curtains. She was relieved to see the door latch in locked position. There was another knock. "Who is it?" No answer. She reached for the curtain, about to peer out, when the door handle moved. Her scalp tingled. Eyes focused on the brief case beside the door. No pistol there tonight. Quietly, she retreated to the bed, knelt, reached beneath it and pulled a long, soft vinyl case toward her. She eased the zipper silently down the length of the gun case and pulled out Mike's short, double-barreled twelve-gauge shotgun. "Barely legal," she had heard him say more than once.

She pushed the lever behind the barrels and the weapon opened. She flinched as another, slightly louder, knock came from the door. She stood up, felt along the top shelf of the closet for two green twelve-gauge shotgun shells she had found in a drawer after moving into Mike and Laura's motor home. Each shell made its own hollow sound when dropped into a barrel. She closed the shotgun, moved quietly to the telephone and dialed 911.

Two Val Verde County sheriff's deputies arrived within ten minutes. They checked under and around the motor home, questioned neighbors, patrolled the RV park with spotlights for half an hour and found nothing. Sarah offered to make coffee for the officers. They declined. She thanked them, then closed and locked the door. She sat down in the small breakfast nook across from the door and stared at the door lock.

What was that all about? Someone at the wrong motor home? Why such a soft knocking? What if she had forgotten to lock the door? She would have been in the shower. Sarah shuddered, stood up and stepped to the refrigerator for a cold bottle of water. She filled half a water tumbler from the bottle. Laura kept bottles of gin, vodka and rum in a padded box in the oven when traveling. Sarah had noticed a large bottle of Maker's Mark bourbon on the oven rack beside the liquor box. She opened the oven door, pulled out the big bottle of whiskey and raised the level of liquid in the tumbler almost to the rim. She turned back to stare at the door as she took two large swallows from the glass. *Did that really happen?* she wondered. She stepped over to the passenger seat and pulled back a corner of the windshield cover. A sheriff's patrol car was parked under the bright streetlights near the entrance of the park. Sarah pushed the cover back in place, turned and took her glass of bourbon to the shower with her.

Just before ten she looked outside again and saw that the patrol car was gone. She closed the window padding again, stepped to the refrigerator and opened its tiny freezer compartment. The struggle for a few cubes of ice from a frozen tray hardly seemed worth it, but the half tumbler of bourbon needed a little chill.

Sarah finished her drink while watching the news on TV, then turned the set off and listened to the darkness for only seconds until she fell asleep. She awakened hours later with a clear impression that she had heard a noise outside. She eased out of bed and moved quietly from window to window with the shotgun, listening, peering out and seeing nothing to alarm her. She returned to bed, wondering again who had knocked at the door earlier and what would have happened if she had forgotten to lock the door.

Her hand tightened on the shotgun at her side. It was heavy and awkward. She missed the little black pistol. Her ex-husband James had bought it for her while they were on their honeymoon in Las Vegas. She missed James, too. He would have been a lifesaver during the last two months but... someone had stolen him, too. James and the pistol, both stolen. Sarah's grip on the shotgun relaxed. There was a very good chance she would be getting her pistol back. No chance at all of getting James back. She fell back asleep.

Ray Summers

6

The next morning, Sarah was seated in the small waiting room at the Mexican port of entry in Ciudad Acuña, Coahuila, Mexico. Traffic entering Mexico from the United States moved slowly past an open double door. Smoke from a Mexican cigarette drifted down the row of seats toward the open doorway.

The distinctive odor caused another person seated there, Customs Special Agent Ryan Shaw, to glance to his left at a dusky young man three seats away. Clean, wide-brimmed straw hat, dark-blue Levi's, white shirt and pristine brown boots hinted that this young man had worked in the U.S. all summer and was now heading home. Ryan guessed he was applying for a permit to take a vehicle registered in the U.S. or other goods past the checkpoint south of town.

The acrid smoke that Ryan merely noticed was the last straw for the strawberry-blonde several seats on the other side of the young Mexican. Mid-thirties, Ryan guessed, attractive enough that she had caught him staring at her twice. She sprang from her seat, fanning invisible smoke with one hand, and bounded to the counter. "Hello... hello, back there." She was tall, her shiny auburn hair short and curly. A baggy long-sleeve shirt and faded oversize jeans gave her a somewhat tousled look. She leaned across the counter, peering toward an open door on her right. The loose jeans tightened, revealing a lean, muscular form. Feeling relatively safe from being caught again, Ryan stared.

"Hello.... *Señor*, I can't wait any longer." She straightened as an official in olive drab emerged from the side door.

"I'm sorry, but I must be going. Yesterday, one of your officers took a pistol from me. I was told that I could pick it up here this morning."

The Mexican official stared at the fair-skinned woman and

smoothed one end of his thick black mustache with his thumb and forefinger.

"Do you understand me? Do you understand English?"

"Wait," the official said, and walked back into the office. Ryan stood, ignoring the feeling that he should not involve himself in this, and walked to the counter. "Excuse me," he almost whispered. "I overheard you say that a pistol was taken from you by a Mexican officer." The woman turned to face him, and Ryan looked down into the bluest eyes he had ever seen. "If that's true," he noticed the freckles and peeling nose, "you were very lucky that you weren't arrested. Bringing firearms into Mexico is a very serious offense. If I were you, I would leave here now, immediately and...."

"Thank you for your concern." The beautiful eyes were glaring. "But please mind your own business."

The officer returned, placing a brown paper bag on the counter. The woman opened the bag and glanced inside. Snatching the bag from the counter, she turned and walked quickly toward the exit. "Thank you," she said over her shoulder as she walked through the open door. Ryan watched as she crossed the street and hurried out of sight without a backward glance.

"And what may I do for you?" the Mexican Customs officer asked.

Ryan pointed toward the smoker. "He was here first."

"What do you want?" the officer shouted to the smoker in Spanish.

The man in new clothes dropped his cigarette and extinguished it with a boot as he stood and hurried to the counter carrying a large brown envelope. Ryan sat down in the nearest front-row seat, wondering how the tousled woman had managed to get a confiscated pistol back from Mexican customs.

Ryan watched the customs officer examine several documents before abruptly shoving them back across the counter, announcing that one of them had not been notarized. The young man in new clothes returned the papers to his envelope, vowed to return shortly and departed. Ryan approached the counter, introduced himself, and presented his credentials.

"Alejandro Villa," the Mexican Customs inspector offered his right hand.

"With much pleasure," Ryan said in Spanish as they shook hands.

Villa fingered the end of his mustache, a patient expression on his face. Again, Ryan spoke in Spanish. "Inspector Villa, there is a woman here in Mexico that I need to speak with. I am told that she works as a cook and housekeeper for the Customs inspectors at the dam. If she is agreeable, I would like permission to take a statement from her."

Inspector Villa frowned. "I cannot give this permission." He moved to the end of the counter, raised a hinged section and motioned Ryan behind the counter. "*El Jefe*, the chief inspector, must give approval. He will not be here today, but I will take the information." He led the way into a small office, signaling Ryan to follow and then take a chair in front of a large, ornate wooden desk. Villa seated himself behind the desk, turned to a fresh page on a yellow legal pad and began writing. A moment later, he looked up. "What is the name of this woman?"

"Arispe, Elvia Arispe-Lorenzo."

Inspector Villa wrote, showing no sign of recognition. "And she works at the dam?"

"Yes." Ryan leaned back in the chair, uncomfortably certain that he would not enjoy answering the next question. With absolutely no authority in Mexico, he would have to answer it and hang out the Customs dirty laundry if he wanted this witness. The question came.

"Why do you want to talk to this woman?"

He wanted this witness. "We have reports that one of our customs inspectors has forced several women to remove their clothing while he watched. He has molested some of them. I believe he has done this to Elvia Arispe. I would like to talk to her about it."

Villa looked up from his legal pad, waiting.

Obviously such a simple explanation would not suffice. Ryan continued. "The inspector pretends to find contraband or says he has information about someone matching the description of the woman he has decided to search. He takes her into a back room and makes her undress."

"And he did this to the woman, Arispe?"

"That's what I have been told."

Villa cocked his head and looked pensive.

"Another inspector reported the incident," Ryan added, hoping to defuse speculation that the Mexican woman had complained.

Villa frowned, as if wondering about the real reason a U.S. Customs agent wanted to see this woman.

Choosing something that Villa and his *jefe* might relate to, Ryan added, "One of the molested women is the granddaughter of a United States senator."

Villa's eyes widened. He nodded, scribbled something on the pad and underlined it. "I will give this information to E*l Jefe*."

Ryan stood up. "I'll come back tomorrow."

"Si, tomorrow."

Ryan knew better than to ask for a time. He would check in the morning but expected nothing before tomorrow afternoon. He thanked the inspector and left. Outside, he crossed the busy southbound traffic lane and boarded the green shuttle bus headed north across the international bridge.

At the Del Rio port of entry, bus passengers were required to leave the bus and pass through a pedestrian lane for U.S. Customs and Immigration inspection. After inspection, passengers returned to the bus now bound for downtown Del Rio, Texas. Ryan didn't reboard the bus but remained at the port, entered a large waiting room on the Immigration side of the port building and walked directly to a glass door marked Officer in Charge. He had been promised a copy of the immigration officer's statement that had sent him seeking the Mexican woman.

Earlier that morning, Port Director Griffin had introduced him to Immigration Officer in Charge Jim Hall. Hall apologized for not meeting them the day before. "A long weekend," he explained. After other brief amenities, Hall closed the office door and stepped to a nearby file cabinet. "The port of entry at the dam is open sixteen hours a day, eight a.m. until midnight," the OIC explained as he examined several file folders. "A Customs inspector and an Immigration inspector are on duty at all times during both eight-hour shifts." When he turned from the file cabinet, he had a manila folder in his hand. "This is the statement of one of my inspectors, Philip Greene, who was working four-to-midnight with Banner when these incidents occurred." Hall tossed the folder onto his desk.

"According to Greene, Banner took the women into the search room alone, so he didn't actually see what went on. None of the women made a formal complaint... as far as we know." Hall and Griffin exchanged agreeable looks. "But according to Greene, all of the women left angry, except for the Hispanic girl... she was crying when she came out of the search room."

Ryan glanced through the report quickly, noting that one woman was from Mexico, a cook and housekeeper for Mexican Customs inspectors at the dam. Ten years ago Ryan would have simply driven into Mexico and talked to the woman. But Mexican authorities were touchy about their turf now. Authorization from Mexican Customs would be necessary before approaching this woman. Acquiring that authorization could be simple, difficult or impossible, depending on local attitudes. Before finishing the Immigration inspector's memorandum, Ryan knew his first act on getting a statement would be to start things moving with authorities south of the border.

Now he was back, with no statement, no authorization, but the initial shot had been fired. He tapped on the glass door and entered when the OIC motioned him in. Jim Hall was standing behind his wide gray government desk. Except for a tan file folder, the desk was clean. Leaning forward, he pushed the folder toward Ryan. "A copy of Greene's statement, his work schedule for the month, home and work phone numbers for him... and me. He will be at the dam this week, early shift." Hall removed his dark-blue suit coat, draped it on a wooden hanger and hung it on a nearby wall rack. "Any luck across the river?"

"Not much. *El Jefe* is out. Won't be back today." Ryan smiled.

Hall shook his head. "A month ago, Griffin and I could have helped you out, but there's been a purge over there." Hall nodded toward Ciudad Acuña. "Neither one of us knows any of the new regime."

Ryan raised his eyebrows.

"It's gambling casinos this time." The OIC motioned Ryan into a chair as he sat down behind his desk. "A group from Mexico City finally got the go-ahead for a few trial casinos out at the lake. There's been talk about it for years, developing the Mexican side of Lake Amistad into a little Las Vegas with water frontage."

Ryan pulled the unmarked folder toward him as the OIC explained local Mexican opposition to Mexico City factions moving in on local parkland: the recent shake-up that replaced heads of almost every federal agency in Ciudad Acuña with people from the interior. Ryan nodded, a weak attempt at feigning interest. Local Mexican politics was no concern of his. In a day or two, he would be back at the Law Enforcement Training Center in D.C., attempting to get a fifteen-week Spanish course for Customs agents off the ground. Budget cuts had dashed hopes for the language lab package he had proposed, but there was still a possibility.

The training center was also where the State Department had expert instructors on tap and a state-of-the-art language lab. For the past month, Ryan had been swimming laps at the training center's Olympic-size pool with the director of the academy. Last Wednesday, she had agreed to dinner Saturday night. He had planned a little club-hopping and dancing. Instead, he had spent Saturday night with the commissioner of customs and the senator. He had to wrap up this little border chore and get back to work.

Ryan's eyes focused on the open folder in front of him. In addition to the Mexican woman, there had been three other victims: A local teenager, identified by Greene; a young woman accompanied by a local high-school football player, identified by Greene. The third woman was driving a Ford Ranchero with New Mexico license plates. Greene had furnished the plate number. The Albuquerque office would run that down for him, come up with name, address, maybe a phone number. This memo from Immigration Inspector Greene was dated two months ago. Ryan was wondering why no action had been taken when something Hall said caught his ear. "The mayor?" he blurted out as he looked up. What had Hall just said about the mayor of Ciudad Acuña?

"Disappeared out on the lake sometime over the weekend," Hall said. "No sign of him or his thirty-two-foot sailboat."

"Bad weather?"

Hall seemed puzzled at Ryan's question. "Beautiful weekend." His mouth tightened. "The popular consensus is that the mayor's disappearance had something to do with his opposition to the casinos. As I just said, he was their most outspoken critic."

Ryan nodded, deciding not to risk comment or question. He should have been paying attention. The OIC had been a tremendous help. Scooping up the folder, Ryan stood. "I'd better get moving on this. Thanks very much for everything." He shook hands and made a quick exit. Crossing the road to the agent's office, he wondered how a boat that size could disappear on a calm inland lake, even a large one like Amistad, and leave no trace. Puzzling, he thought, but certainly no concern of his.

Ray Summers

7

Sarah pulled the can of Diet Pepsi from her small ice chest and sat down on the cushioned port-side seat of the Boston Whaler. Arching her back and rolling her shoulders, she leaned back and sipped the ice-cold drink as the big Johnson outboard gurgled quietly at idle speed. She was satisfied with the day's effort. Abandoning her own search for the day, she had concentrated on contacting the Mexican search teams. Some of them would still be searching the lake long after she had returned to New Mexico. She found that almost every team was already in possession of at least one of her Spanish-language flyers. The *federale* in charge of the search had kept his word about distributing them. He had also kept his word about the return of her pistol.

The boat drifted past one of the white buoys marking the international boundary in this open stretch of water. There were twenty-eight of the numbered, red-blinking markers located to show the original meandering channel of the Rio Grande. There was no common distance separating them, but by now Sarah knew that the number on the buoy closely approximated the number of miles it was from Amistad Dam. This one was number seventeen, which translated to a good hour-and-a-half run back to the Pecos Bridge boat ramp twenty miles northwest. Sarah glanced westward at the late afternoon sun. There would be time to look at the cove again. The Mexican searchers had radios. If any of them were there she could find out if anyone or anything had been found.

Sarah stood up, removed her dark sunglasses and squinted at a distant dot on the open water. Stepping to the steering console, she sat the cold drink down, picked up the binoculars and raised them to eye level. The object was a small green square-bowed jon boat, a type in common use by commercial trotline fishermen on the Mexican side of the lake. As usual, this one was occupied by only one person, someone wearing a bright blue cap. What wasn't usual was to see a Mexican commercial fisherman drifting in deep open water. Perhaps he was in trouble, Sarah thought. That was the direction she was going. Replacing the binoculars and donning the sunshades, she picked up her drink and pushed the throttle forward.

As the Boston Whaler surged toward it, the fishing boat immediately moved westward, toward the Mexican shoreline. Obviously not in any trouble. Sarah put it out of her mind. The half-dozen permanent fishing camps had been her first priority for inquiries about her sister when she learned of them. Chango had been very helpful there. As he was the owner of the fishing rights for the Mexican portion of Lake Amistad, they were legally his camps.

There seemed to be a unique arrangement between Chango and the occupants of each camp. Chango accounted for supplies and groceries sold by his lakeside convenience-store-cum-bar-and-grill to the fishermen against credit for fresh fish they delivered with figures scribbled on cardboard boxes, scraps of paper, palms of hands, even scratched out in the ground. Sarah had never witnessed a fisherman dispute Chango's accounting, though at times some appeared dismayed with the outcome. Chango had taken her to all of the camps and introduced her to practically every fisherman. She had been to the fishing camps many times now. All the trotliners were aware of the one-hundred dollars reward for information about Laura and Mike. That is what she had given the fisherman who had found Laura's cap, and word of it had reached the fishing camps ahead of her or her flyers. She wanted to offer more, but Chango had advised to stay with the hundred dollars, saying that amount would be believable to the fishermen.

The two miles of open water between the Mexican and U.S. shorelines slowly narrowed to a quarter of that distance, funneling her into a westward turn, then south, completing the first one-hundred-eighty-degree bend of an almost perfect twenty-mile-long S-curve that would eventually leave her again pointed northward. Adjusting boat speed for what was now a southward run against the choppy whitecaps, she took the last drink of Diet Pepsi, looked at the empty can and thought of her fuel supply.

Running a five-gallon supply can dry sometimes made it difficult to restart the motor, and she had been running from the same first can all day. With everything clear ahead, and two hundred yards of water on each side, she moved from the console to the stern, disconnected the small dual-pressure fuel hose from the gasoline can feeding the eighty-five-horse outboard and plugged it into a full can. As she returned to the steering wheel, the motor suddenly stopped. The bow of the boat settled and, pointed into the wind, all headway ceased almost immediately. Soon the boat was drifting back the way it had come.

Sarah's first thought was that she had plugged into an already-empty fuel can, but she had filled all four cans on her way home from the Mexican marina last night. Her next thought was how quiet it was, only the sound of whitecaps slapping against the fiberglass hull. Somehow, an unsettling sound in a powerless boat.

She moved to the stern, hefted the connected gasoline can. It was full. Some glitch inside the can? She knew that one of the small hoses in the double line supplied light pressure from the motor to the fuel can, forcing gasoline through the other hose to run the motor. The trouble must be the can, she reasoned. She switched the hose connection to another full can of fuel, squeezed the rubber bulb in the fuel line, pumping fuel toward the motor the way she always did after running a tank dry. The battery was less than two months old. It turned the motor effortlessly, again and again, producing not a single sputter from the motor. Sarah pumped the rubber bulb again, then thought perhaps she had pumped it too much the first time. She waited, studying the empty lake and the desolate rocky shoreline on either side. She knew all too well that the only human habitation within twenty miles was one of the Mexican fishing camps, three, maybe four miles around the next bend. The bend itself was still a good four miles away – against the wind.

She pushed the starter button again, this time moving the throttle back and forth as the outboard cycled repeatedly without firing. Sarah took her finger off the button and took a deep breath. There couldn't be something wrong with both almost-new gas cans. What then? She checked her drift against a distant rocky outcrop. She seemed to be remaining in the main channel, moving slowly northward, back the way she had come, not toward either shore. Where were all the boats? Where were all the searchers she had seen all day?

She picked up the binoculars and scanned the lake behind her. One of the small green fishing boats came into view from the bend she had passed some ten minutes ago. One person, of course... wearing a bright blue cap. It was the same fisherman she had seen earlier. She felt instant relief, put the glasses down and walked to the front of the boat, checking the coiled bowline to be sure it wasn't tangled. The small jon boat would have difficulty towing a larger craft against the stiff breeze. She would probably have to beach the Whaler and return with someone tomorrow to either fix it or tow it in. At least she wouldn't be spending the night on the lake. The fisherman would take her on to the boat ramp where her Ranchero was parked.

When she looked again, the small boat was nowhere in sight. Sarah raised the binoculars, panning the lake and shorelines. Several inlets off the channel near the bend offered possible reasons for the boat's sudden disappearance. It was across the mouths of such coves that the fishermen strung lines of baited hooks. Sarah put the binoculars down and stepped back to the rear starboard bench seat. She raised the hinged cushion, opening a storage area. This was where the Weavers stored emergency equipment: fire extinguisher, first-aid kit, snakebite kit, flashlight, batteries, a small ax, Coleman lantern and fuel and distress flares. She picked up the small package of flares, placed them on top of the steering console and lowered the seat. When the fisherman came back into view, she would make sure he saw her.

She glanced again in the direction she had last seen him and raised the binoculars. Nothing on the right, only the mouth of two small inlets and a sloping, rocky beach. She panned across the half-mile of white-capped water to the western shoreline. Three large inlets, a quarter-mile apart with low brown-rock cliffs in between. She went back to the middle niche. It would have been straight ahead of the boat rounding the bend. The blue cap caught her eye. A man was sitting cross-legged atop the cliffs bordering the near side of the inlet. His hands were raised to his face; binoculars stared back at her. Sarah lowered her glasses, blinked in surprise, then removed her wide-brimmed hat and waved it at the distant cliffs. Returning the glasses to her eyes, she continued waving, but saw no acknowledgement from the man looking on. Sarah replaced her hat and sighted through the binoculars along the cliff line until the cliffs became rubble, then a narrow rocky beach. There was the green jon boat, its small outboard-motor propeller raised above the water. Sarah moved the glasses back along the cliff. When she found the man in the blue cap again, she noticed a rifle lying across his folded legs. Now what was a Mexican fisherman doing with a rifle? She moved the glasses back to the beached boat. For that matter, what was a Mexican fisherman doing on the U.S. side of the lake? Sarah lowered the binoculars, thinking, *if not a fisherman, then who? A deer poacher?* She considered that, reasoning that trot-liners probably didn't eat fish all the time, not with venison available for the taking and deer so plentiful on the U.S. side. Sarah put the binoculars down. She would wait for the wind to carry her nearer, then use one of the paddles to steer the boat into the cove.

She stared at the four fuel tanks. What could possibly be wrong? She had made that switch dozens of times. Maybe it was the connector. She moved to the rear of the boat again, knelt, unfastened and reconnected the hoses. The brass, two-pronged connector seemed to fit perfectly. The cap on the fuel can seemed tight. Maybe the air vent was blocked. She unscrewed the cap. The motion of the rolling boat sloshed liquid from the overfilled can onto Sarah's hand. She quickly replaced the cap and tightened it. She didn't need gasoline on her already-ravaged hands.

She pulled a roll of paper towels from a nearby compartment under the seat and dried her hand. Realizing she smelled no gasoline, she raised her hand and sniffed. Nothing. She sniffed again, then raised the crumpled towel and sniffed again. Still nothing. She knelt, unscrewed the filler cap again, and dipped half of the twisted paper towel into the can.

The towel came out dripping. Again she smelled of it. Absolutely nothing. This can was full of water. How could that be? She had filled all four gas cans last night herself, measured and poured the required amount of oil into the three empty cans and the half-empty one, then filled all four with gasoline. She stared unbelievingly at the red oblong five-gallon fuel cans. They were hers, no doubt about that, two old ones with dents, scratches and peeling paint and the two new ones, still sporting the dealer's price stickers. She uncapped the other two full cans and found that they also contained water.

She straightened, backing slowly away from the open sloshing cans, trying to fathom what was going on and becoming very frightened. Who had emptied the cans and refilled them with water? And why? Obviously, the cans weren't the objective. They were easy and fast targets for outright theft.

The steering console stopped her slow unconscious retreat from the water-filled fuel cans. She looked up. She had drifted closer to the cliffs and the inlet where the small boat was beached, but with the naked eye she couldn't make out the man or his blue cap. She picked up the binoculars and tried to find him but couldn't, yet the boat was still there. She moved the glasses back to the cliffs, raising them slightly to view the higher sloping terrain beyond. The cenizo-covered hillside had begun to take on a late-afternoon glow. Sarah looked back along the cliffs and spotted the blue cap.

The man had moved nearer, some fifty yards closer, to a new location. He was again seated, leaning forward, elbows braced on his knees, binoculars aimed in her direction, rifle leaning against a small outcrop of rock beside him. Why was he still watching her? Suddenly, she was again aware of the soft tapping sound of the small waves against the hull. A chill went through her. For an instant she didn't know why, then it came to her: the tapping at her door last night, like waves against the boat, then later, something had awakened her... someone replacing the gas in her fuel cans in the boat with water? Her whole being went cold. This man on the cliffs was waiting for her. Sarah lowered the binoculars and gauged the distance now separating her from the waiting man. Still a quarter of a mile at least, but the wind was taking her directly toward him. He must have followed her all day, waiting for her to run the first tank dry... but she hadn't run it dry – not yet anyway. She moved quickly to the fuel cans, hefted the one she had been using all day, grimaced at its lightness, plugged the hose into it and pumped the primer bulb.

Placing the throttle in normal starting position, she looked toward the cliffs and pushed the starter button. The motor made its helpless whirring, cycling sound. In the distance, Sarah could now see the blue cap without binoculars, a speck in the brown and gray just above the water line. Still pressing the starter button, she reached over and placed her left hand on the throttle. There would be water inside the motor now, wherever the fuel was supposed to be. Would it be better to let more fuel in or just keep cranking? Still staring at the blue dot on the cliffs, she pushed the throttle forward. The motor kept making its whirring sound that signaled it wasn't starting.

Sarah glanced quickly at the shorelines on either side. The one on her right, eastward, was the nearest. She was a good swimmer and could cover the two hundred yards of open water easily enough. But that was Mexico, and the shoreline of a peninsula, five miles long, maybe one mile wide, aptly named *La Bolsa*, the pocket. The other shoreline, the U.S., was the eastern edge of another, similar-sized peninsula jutting southward. The man with the rifle would only have to move up the slope behind him to cut her off from the mainland. The Mexican side was her best chance. When she hit the water, the man would return to his boat and try to intercept her, but she was sure she could make it to shore and into the rocks. Then what? *Run* was all she could think of now, *just run*.

The Johnson eighty-five-horse outboard fired, sputtered and died. Sarah pulled the throttle back to the start mark and pressed harder on the black button. The motor fired again, sputtered, fired and began to shudder. Puffs of thick white smoke drifted past her as she let up on the starter. She turned to look at the motor. Smoke streaming over the transom began to thin, motor vibration diminished, and the boat began to move. Sarah faced forward and straightened the boat, pointing it due south. Slowly she advanced the throttle to cruising speed and didn't look back.

She was not going to make the twenty remaining miles to the Pecos Bridge boat ramp. The thirsty outboard would suck the fuel can dry long before then. The man in the blue cap would know that... and would not be far behind.

Sarah reached for her briefcase. The small pistol inside would be of little use against a rifle; she was still glad it was there. She opened the thick briefcase, took out the pistol and shoved it in her waistband. Her large geological-survey map of the Amistad Recreation Area had been confiscated by the Mexican officer who took her weapon. But there was another one with the emergency items, far simpler and less detailed.
Sarah stood up, one hand on the steering wheel, and leaned over and raised the bench-seat cushion to open a storage compartment. The map did show the surrounding topography she would soon be traversing on foot.

A can of Coleman lantern fuel stored in the compartment immediately caught her attention. If that gasoline burned in a lantern, it should burn in a motor. Sarah pulled the throttle back to just above idle and emptied the gallon can of lantern fuel into the boat's fuel supply. Maybe she wouldn't need the map after all. The Coleman fuel might get her as far as Seminole Canyon, out of the river channel and within walking distance of the state-park camping area.

8

It was dusk when Ryan turned off the highway onto the side street that allowed access to the rear parking area of the Ramada Inn. His ground-level room was on the southeast corner facing a huge unpaved parking lot that thus far contained only two eighteen-wheelers, their refrigeration units plugged into outlets on a bordering wooden fence. Ryan maneuvered past them to the blacktop strip in front of the rooms and parked. He pulled his briefcase from the rear seat, got out and walked toward his room. The briefcase contained fourteen-year-old Lupe Martinez's statement on tape.

It had happened with her almost the same as with Jill Cowden, except Lupe had refused to take off her clothes. When Banner tried to do it for her, she screamed. He backed off and allowed her to leave the search room. The boyfriend, who had been ordered by Banner to wait in the car, had since returned to college in Austin. He could be found and his statement taken by agents from the nearest office to Austin. Ryan would make that request in the morning. His immediate plans were to take a shower, grab a bite to eat at the motel restaurant and make another attempt at telephoning the California woman.

Inspector Greene hadn't recognized the girl accompanying young Mark Simms, offensive left tackle for the Del Rio Rams high school football team. Greene's memo said Customs Inspector Banner took the girl into the search room at 10 p.m. on June 14, while Mark remained in the pickup. The girl returned 15 minutes later, and the couple drove away. According to Greene's memo, Mark Simms worked at his father's Texaco station on Avenue F during the summer. Greene had listed the telephone number. Ryan called the number.

Mark said that he and his friend, Marsha Horton, hadn't

complained or told anyone about Marsha having to take off her clothes because they were in his father's new pickup that wasn't supposed to be taken into Mexico. Marsha had been visiting relatives in Del Rio for the summer but had now returned to San Diego. Mark had her address and telephone number but was concerned about his father finding out where he had driven the pickup. Ryan asked Marsha's age. Mark answered that he thought she was 22. "Don't worry about it," Ryan told him, "Give me her phone number, and you're out of it." That conversation had taken place two hours and three phone calls ago. So far, there had been no answer at Marsha's number.

As Ryan entered the motel lobby, he stopped at the front desk to check for messages. Maybe the Albuquerque office had called with something on the woman in the Ranchero. The clerk handed him a slip with a local number on it.

Once in his room, Ryan tossed the briefcase onto a bed, removed his suit coat and dropped it atop the briefcase. He sat down on the bed, picked up the phone headset and punched in the number.

Customs Agent Tom Del Castillo answered. He said he was having a "little cookout" at his home. "Fajitas are going on the grill right now and there's plenty of cold beer. Come on out."

"Sounds just great," Ryan replied. "Where?"

"North of town, same way you and Henderson went yesterday. Two miles past the 'Y,' take a right through the stone entryway, Laguna Verde Estates; fifth street down the road is cenizo Way. Hang a left at the sign and we're at the end of the street."

♦　♦　♦

The thick columns of the entryway were built of local reddish-brown limestone. Fortress-like wooden fences of the same material stretched outward from the columns. Lighter-colored stones spelled LAGUNA on the left column and VERDE on the right one. The windows were broken on a wooden-security station hut that occupied an island just inside the entrance. Past the dark checkpoint, two lanes of patched asphalt stretched into the darkness. Encroaching weeds and brush left no shoulders along the rough pavement. The deterioration indicated how the housing-community developer's dreams had hit a fiscal roadblock.

Ryan brightened the headlights as he approached the first intersection. To his left, a metal pole supporting a faded green street sign reading Buckthorn Drive protruded from a large, impenetrable huisache thicket. Ryan pulled into the intersection and looked into the darkness on either side. Not a house or light in sight. It seemed no one lived on Buckthorn Drive or anywhere else in Laguna Verde that he could see. He drove on: Manzanita Drive, Chokecherry Lane, Mesquite Trail, all equally forsaken. At the next intersection he turned left onto Cenizo Way and drove toward a lone distant glow in the darkness.

The light source came from behind a large two-story home opposite the cul-de-sac entrance. It was the only visible residence on Cenizo Way. Ryan parked on the street behind three other cars and got out. The aroma of wood smoke and roasting meat greeted him like an old friend. He inhaled deeply and looked up at the moonless sky. It was clear and bright. Ryan was certain that every star that had ever existed was now back in place. Only in the Arizona and Texas outlands had he seen skies like this. He stared a moment longer before turning toward the house.

There was movement behind a low fence between the backlit house and its detached garage. *Around here*, a silhouette beckoned. Ryan walked up the sloping driveway past a covered boat on a trailer. The slender shadow materializing in jeans, dark T-shirt and white sneakers opened a short wrought-iron gate and offered a hand. "Hank Bishop, ATF."

"Ryan Shaw, Customs." Ryan stepped through the gate and shook Hank's hand.

The backyard was large, lighted by an antique three-globed streetlight set in the center of a thick, closely clipped lawn. The soft light exposed the delicious-smelling haze that Ryan had detected from the street.

"Beer's over here." Bishop led the way to a covered Spanish-tiled patio extending from the rear of the house. Pausing under the low roof, he dropped an empty beer can into a waste container, leaned over and raised the lids on two large ice chests. "Coors and Bud in here." He straightened with another silver can in his hand. "Not sure about that one." He indicated the other ice chest and popped the tab on his beer. Ryan leaned down, cleared ice away and selected a brown bottle. He twisted off the cap and drank. He was partial to strong-flavored Mexican beer. Bohemia had just the right bite.

At the far end of the patio, past a long wooden table, Tom Del Castillo saluted with his own brown bottle. "Glad you could make it." He drank and continued turning strips of meat on the large brick barbecue pit before him. Smoke drifted across the yard, almost obscuring a woman and two men facing the darkness beyond a waist-high stone fence. One of the men aimed a rifle into the blackness.

"Tom dragged all his toys out for us." Bishop nodded toward the others at the fence and led the way. The man aiming the rifle lowered it and commented, "That's a heavy son-of-a-bitch," as he passed the weapon to the man beside him.

"Eleven and a half pounds fully loaded," Ryan volunteered as he and Bishop approached. The woman and two men turned to face them. Young, Ryan thought. None of them, Bishop included, could possibly be more than twenty-five. Dressed in jeans, short-sleeve shirts, and sports shoes, each had the glow of a little too much sun. Evidently, they had spent another day on the lake.

"Ryan Shaw," Bishop began the introductions, "this is Don Sutton, Gary Fulbright, Anita Crouse."

Ryan shook hands with Don, the smallest of the three men. He had short blond hair and large dark eyes. Gary was of medium height with receding dark hair. Ryan noticed that he had kept the barrel of the Army rifle pointed safely skyward as he pivoted. "Eleven and a half pounds, huh?" Gary offered his hand. "Another M-1 Garand buff?"

"No," Ryan shook hands, "but I had an old supervisor who claimed he had dragged one all over Europe during World War II. He had one issued to his agents in Nogales and put every man under him through boot-camp rifle training." Ryan turned to the pretty female agent. Anita could not possibly be out of high school. Short, nice figure, dark curly hair, no visible makeup. Ryan approved of her natural look and the fact that the model 1911 .45 she was waving around had the slide locked back. She turned, placed the pistol on a blanket draped across the brick wall, then turned back to shake hands. "We're thinking about getting a search warrant for this place." She smiled and tilted her head toward the short brick wall behind her.

Ryan had already noticed the armament laid out on the blanket: four revolvers, two semi-automatic pistols, two scoped rifles and two shotguns. A sizable collection, but Ryan had seen larger ones among law-enforcement officers.

"They wouldn't let me into the Aryan Brotherhood," Tom joked from the patio. "So I'm starting my own group." He chuckled.

A petite Hispanic woman dressed in dark brown slacks and a white blouse appeared from the house carrying two large serving bowls. A young boy of eight or nine years followed with a covered platter. The bowls and platter were arranged on the long wooden patio table. Tom motioned everyone toward him, "Come and get it."

Ryan introduced himself to Isabel, Tom's wife, and their son, Jimmy, as he helped himself to the food. He could feel the tenderness of the fajitas as he pushed the large serving fork into them. Wrapped in freshly made flour tortillas with homemade salsa and pico de gallo, they were delicious.

Dinner-conversation topics, often several at the same time, drifted from the savory food back to Tom's arsenal, then to a green Volkswagen Beetle that Tom evidently had ordered towed from under the Pecos River bridge.

"Registered to B.E. Patterson in Amarillo," Tom said. "No stolen report on it. Must be broke down." Tom looked at Ryan. "We don't want anybody showing up to pick it up or work on it in the middle of our deal."

Ryan nodded and allowed the subject to drop. A location for delivery of the machine guns had apparently been selected, probably the date and time also. He didn't want to know any of it. "You have a beautiful home," he said turning to Isabel.

"Thank you." She smiled.

"It's pretty nice," Tom said, glancing around. "It was the model home for this subdivision. The developer hoped the lake nearby would drive sales, but over the years it took for it to fill up he made no sales and his financing ran out." Tom shrugged. "The development went bankrupt and I got a very sweet deal on it." He took a large bite of fajita and shook his head.

"Now that the lake is full a couple of lots just got sold," Isabel noted. "We won't be able to host shooting parties much longer. We've been here four years."

"Well, it's a beautiful home," Anita said. "Fantastic compared to my tiny one-bedroom apartment in north Houston, and there's no traffic problem here."

Everyone chuckled. Rush-hour traffic between Houston and its suburbs then emerged as the new conversation topic. Ryan had nothing to contribute. A small room in a back-street hotel within walking distance of the Embassy in downtown Madrid had served as his base camp for more than eight years. A place to catch up on sleep and have his wardrobe serviced between trips. That was all he needed, at least now.

Ryan looked at Isabel and Jimmy. He wouldn't have those as subject matter either. Conversations would move to discussions of families any time now. Marriage had never happened for him, but he carried scars from times when it could have.

He'd become close with Mary, and often imagined what might have been if they had married. His interest had been piqued again two years ago by the enchanting Yolanda, whom he met when he signed on undercover with a cocaine-smuggling scheme via an old border canyon route while he was looking for his friend and onetime fellow agent Grady Matthews, who went missing near the border farther west in Texas. She was the granddauther of Don Lalo Naranjo, a longtime border drug smuggler. Not longer after he and Yolanda had romantically connected, she disappeared to places unknown. But his memory of her still lingered.

"Are you here for the machine guns too?" Isabel asked. Ryan hadn't realized he had been staring at her.

"No, something else." He looked away, thinking how rude it was of him to stare and how short his answer had been.

"He's going to get 'Magic Fingers' for us," Tom said.

"Magic Fingers?" Anita raised her narrow, unmarked eyebrows.

"Magic Fingers." Tom's gaze swept the table. "One of our fine upstanding Customs inspectors. He likes to fondle women while pretending to search their purses."

Everyone stopped eating and listened.

"Magic Fingers?" Gary repeated.

"That's what the other inspectors call him," Tom answered.

"And none of the women complain?" Anita asked.

"He picks the young ones who are afraid," Isabel answered.

"He takes them into the search room out at the dam and makes them strip," Tom added.

"You mean a male inspector..." Anita began.

"Hey," Tom interrupted. "I bet you know him." He surveyed the table again. "We got him from you, he came from ATF in Houston – Chuck Banner."

"Banner!" Gary lowered his can of beer and exchanged looks with Hank.

"I thought you might know him." Tom smiled.

"Oh, we know him, alright," Hank said. "What a..." He glanced across the table at Jimmy. "...arrogant jerk. I knew he was not overly bright, but I didn't know he was a pervert."

"Vindictive," Gary added. "When he heard he wasn't going to make probation, that ATF was going to dump him, he filed grievances against every supervisor in the Houston office and a civil suit against the agent in charge. He had the entire office tied up for weeks answering phony charges."

Don smiled and looked at Tom. "Then you guys grabbed him." He laughed and took a long swallow of beer.

"I've heard stories about him," Anita sighed, "but he was before my time."

"Are you with Internal Affairs?" Hank's question focused everyone's attention on Ryan.

"No, I'm here on what you might call a special assignment."

"Headquarters sent him," Tom volunteered from the end of the table. "Banner strip searched a U.S. senator's granddaughter last Thursday night."

Ryan noticed Isabel glance down at her son. Jimmy had stopped eating and was all ears.

Ryan shifted in his chair. It had been interesting, actually very informative up to this point, but he would not add fuel to the rumor mill. "I have to make a phone call, credit card," he said. "Maybe Jimmy can show me where the telephone is." He looked at Tom. Tom nodded and Jimmy sprang from his chair. Ryan followed him into the house, through the kitchen and down a hallway to a darkened room. Jimmy flipped the light switch on.

The den was large. Heavy, dark beams supported a high ceiling of knotty-pine planking. One windowless wall was lined with shelves of books. Indian artifacts and Charles Russell and Frederic Remington western scene prints adorned the other walls. End tables of dark wood plus a blanket motif sofa and chairs completed the rustic look.

Ryan examined a frame of flint arrow points displayed on a nearby wall. "Did you find these?"

"Some of them," Jimmy replied. "Phone's over there." He pointed toward the wall of bookshelves across the room, and then rushed to the dark table at the end of the sofa. "I have some that I found this summer." He pulled open a shallow drawer in the table. "We haven't mounted them yet."

Ryan paused on his way to the telephone and examined half a dozen flint points that Jimmy held in the palm of his hand. Ryan selected the largest. "A pink one, and it's perfect," Ryan commented holding the arrowhead at arms length.

Some types of chert change colors when they're heated. The Indians did that sometimes to make it easier to work."

Ryan stared down at the boy. "How old are you?"

"Almost ten."

"Where did you learn so much about making arrowheads?"

"Dad told me, and I have lots of artifact books."

Ryan nodded. His gaze moved to a small cardboard box inside the open drawer. "What are those?"

"Fossil snails... see?" Jimmy handed Ryan what appeared to be a gray, gumball-size stone. Ryan studied the fossil, turning it between forefinger and thumb. It was indeed a petrified snail.

"They're from the Cretaceous period, sixty-six to one-hundred-forty-four million years ago," Jimmy said.

Ryan nodded again and replaced the specimen.

"We found lots of them last summer. They're the big clue to finding the Lost Caracol Mine."

Ryan smiled. "The Lost Caracol Mine? So you're a treasure hunter, too?"

"We're going to find it." Jimmy reached into the drawer, pulled out a manila file folder and brought it to Ryan. "My dad and I joined a treasure hunters' club that sent us information on the Lost Caracol gold mine. It's here, not far from Del Rio. Dad and I started looking for it this summer."

Ryan opened the folder and glanced at the report, the arrowheads on the table, the box of snail fossils, and the boy beaming up at him. Tom Del Castillo already had his treasure. "Jimmy, I want to hear more about the arrowheads and the lost mine, but first I have to take care of this phone call." He handed back the folder.

"Sure," Jimmy smiled, put away the arrow points and folder and closed the drawer, and hurried toward the door. "I'll be outside." Terrific kid, Ryan thought.

The credit-card call to San Diego was answered on the third ring. "Hello." The raspy voice sounded female.

"Miss Horton?"

"Speaking."

The high-school football player had said Marsha was twenty-two. She sounded older. Ryan identified himself and said, "I'm calling from Del Rio, Texas. I understand you recently spent some time here."

After a brief silence, Marsha Horton said, "Who is this again? And what's this about?" She sounded annoyed.

"I'm a special agent with the U.S. Customs Service. I'm calling to find out if you were mistreated when you and Mark Simms returned from Mexico at the Amistad Dam port of entry."

Another silence, then, "Have you talked to Mark?"

"Yes. He gave me your name and phone number." Ryan paused for a moment. "His father still doesn't know about his pickup being in Mexico. I'm interested in what happened after the inspector took you inside the building. If you can help me out with that, I can leave Mark out of it."

"Well, I don't want Mark to get into any trouble. Going across was my idea. Del Rio is a dull place and so is... whatever that place is across the river."

"Ciudad Acuña," Ryan filled in. "You drove out to the casinos and came back across the dam. What happened there?"

"No big deal, really. The officer made us get out of the pickup while he looked inside. I noticed right away that he was more interested in me than the truck. Then he went inside the building. We could see through the window that he typed something into a computer, waited for an answer, then came back out and said I had to go inside."

Ryan heard her take a deep breath. The rest of the story came in singsong cadence. "He took me inside, said I matched a description in the computer and I would have to be strip-searched before he could let us go, and there was no female inspector on duty at the dam so we would have to wait for one to come from town." She took another breath. "I knew that was bullshit and told him so. Then he holds up a bottle of pills he claimed he found in the truck. That was bullshit, too. We argued about the pills for a few minutes. I knew what he wanted, so I said OK, went into another room with him, pulled down my pants, gave him a good look and he let us go. No big deal."

Now it was Ryan's turn to take a deep breath. He had questions, but they could wait until he had a recorder going. Ryan glanced at his watch. "Can I call you back in about an hour and go over this again? I'd like to record it, have it typed and then send it to you for your signature."

"As long as it doesn't get Mark into trouble. I'll be here till nine or so."

Ryan looked at his watch again, subtracting three hours. He had an hour and a half. He had the tape recorder with him, in the briefcase, but the telephone attachment was in an overnight bag at the motel. "I'll call back in an hour."

"I'll be here."

"Thank you." Ryan hung up, wondering briefly what Marsha might consider a "big deal." He walked to the doorway, turned and admired the den again before flipping off the light switch. He paused in the kitchen. It was also large. Blond hardwood cabinets covered the walls except for the wide window above the sink area. Floor tiles were a shade darker and larger than the tan ones that covered the countertops.

Ryan had never been a homeowner, but from what he had seen of Laguna Verde Estates and information volunteered by his hosts, Tom and Isabel seemed to have lucked out with this one. Possibly a reason an agent with Tom's experience and seniority was still a street agent in Del Rio instead of a resident agent in charge somewhere. Ryan moved on toward the patio door, still looking. The place was beautiful. If you happened to find a house that made a lovely home, and get a great deal on it, this was the one.

Someone outside was making parrot sounds – then laughter. As he stepped out onto the patio, he saw that Gordon Shanks had arrived. Gordon had been assigned the parrot-smuggling case. "Have fun," he said, grabbing a paper plate. "The U.S. attorney has authorized prosecution and," he made his way around the table to the fajita platter, "I just may have all of you called back as witnesses." Gordon forked a strip of beef into his plate and picked up a tortilla on his way to the ice chests. "You want to come back for a parrot-smuggler trial, Mr. Shaw?"

"I think I'll pass," Ryan said as he returned to his seat. This was the first time he could recall a fellow street agent calling him mister. He surveyed the cherub-like faces around him. This is what the commissioner's new super agents were going to look like, and they were all going to call him mister and sir. Had he grown that old overseas? He dismissed the thought.

"Beer, anyone?" Gordon stood over the ice chests.

"Longneck here," Tom raised a hand.

"Coors... and a Bud," Hank said, checking the can in front of Anita. Gordon tossed the canned beer. Hank caught both of them, passing the

Budweiser to Anita. It slipped as she popped the tab, and a geyser of foam shot across the table, dousing Ryan's left shoulder and Jimmy's face. Isabel stripped paper towels from a roll on the table and had her son dry before the laughter subsided.

"Tastes bad." Jimmy made a face as his mother passed the roll of towels to Ryan.

"Was good and cold, though, wasn't it?" Ryan smiled and dabbed his shirt.

Across the table, Anita apologized, picked up her now-almost-empty Budweiser can and took the unopened Coors from Hank's hand. "I'll get us a couple of tame ones." She shot a sour look at Gordon and headed for the ice chests.

"I'm soaked," Ryan said as he stood. The white short-sleeve dress shirt was plastered to his arm and shoulder.

"I have a shirt you can borrow." Tom stood up from the table.

"No thanks. It's time for me to head back to the motel anyway. I have another call to make from there." He thanked Tom and Isabel, and looked down at the boy. "Jimmy, I enjoyed the visit. Sorry I have to rush off." As they shook hands, Jimmy invited him back. So did Tom as he walked Ryan to the gate.

"Good luck with Magic Fingers," someone shouted as Ryan passed through the gate into the darkness. He started the Dodge and retraced his route through the uninhabited subdivision, past the abandoned guard shack and stone columns, pausing on the shoulder of the highway for a pair of approaching headlights. The southbound vehicle flashed past, a red blur in the Dart's low-beam headlights.

Ryan straightened in the seat. Was that a Ford Ranchero? It had been two months since the woman from New Mexico was taken into the search room. No, she wouldn't still be in the area. Ryan checked the highway. Clear to the south, more headlights approaching from the north, but he could make it. He floor-boarded the accelerator, showering the stone pillars with flying gravel. As he closed on the speeding vehicle he saw the bright orange and yellow of a New Mexico license plate.

9

Sarah stopped in front of her dark Winnebago, staring into her Ford's rearview mirror at the headlights that had pulled up behind her. The lights retreated a few feet and stopped. She'd assumed it was another sheriff's patrol car pulling in behind her on the highway. Now she wasn't sure. She should have waited at the lighted entryway to see who was behind her. Where were the deputies who had been following? Sarah moved the gearshift into drive position and was about to release the brake and tromp the accelerator when flashing blue and red lights bounced into the mirror. Sarah moved the gearshift back to park.

When the lantern fuel ran out, she had beached the boat a quarter of a mile from the pictograph shelter in Seminole Canyon. The trail to the campground was well-marked and -maintained. She covered its two miles in total darkness, quietly and quickly. A camper in the state park had offered a ride to the boat ramp, but what might have been waiting for her there? The campground had two pay phones. She tried every number listed for Amistad National Park. By then it was after nine, so there was no answer. She called the Sheriff's Office in Del Rio and two deputies arrived in less than an hour, drove her to the boat ramp, unhitched the boat trailer for her and promised to follow her home.

In the overhead mirror, silhouettes were moving behind the Ranchero and someone was shouting orders. She lowered the driver's window and recognized the voice of the big deputy, Carl. "Keep both hands up, turn around, and kneel."

Sarah turned in the seat. Through the rear window she saw a tall figure turn his back to the patrol car and drop to his knees. Only his head and upraised arms were visible above the lower edge of the rear window.

"Now cross your legs, left ankle over the right," Deputy Carl ordered, and then cautiously approached. He took something from the kneeling man's hand and turned toward the light. The voice of the smaller deputy came from behind the glaring headlights of the kneeling man's vehicle. "He's got a loaded .45 in here."

"It's OK," Carl shouted. "He's a Customs agent." In a quieter voice, Sarah heard him say, "Here, Mr. Shaw, let me help you up. Mind if I ask why...."

"Customs!" Sarah threw open the door, scrambled out and rushed to the rear of the Ranchero. The tall man was now on his feet. He and the deputy turned to face her. Sarah knew instantly that she had seen this man before. She remembered his tallness, the wavy dark hair and, though not visible now because of his squinting, the vivid, animal-like green eyes that had checked her out this morning in the waiting room. Now he had come out of the darkness and followed her home. "Damn it, are all you Customs people perverts?"

The tall man shaded his eyes against the glaring headlights and looked down at her. "Well, hello again," he said, maneuvering until he shaded only one side of his face. The change of position brought an overpowering smell of beer to Sarah.

"My name is Ryan Shaw," the reeking man said in a pleasant voice. "I'm a special agent with the U.S. Customs Service. I'm looking for a lady driving a Ford Ranchero with New Mexico plates who may have had a problem with one of our inspectors."

"I'm the lady, but I didn't have a problem. Your inspector is the one with the problem. Apparently you have one too. You smell like a brewery." She turned and strode toward the motor home.

"I'd like to talk to you about the inspector," she heard him shout after her. "Tomorrow maybe?"

She unlocked the motor home, stepped inside and slammed the door.

Ryan shook his head and turned toward the two deputies. They were staring at him. "I can smell the beer too, Mr. Shaw," the big one said. "Do you have very far to drive?"

"I'm staying at the Ramada and I've only had one beer, honest.

Somebody spilled one on me... out at Tom Del Castillo's house. Do you know Tom?"

"Yeah, we know Tom." The big deputy looked at his partner, then back to Ryan. "Just take it easy back to the motel. We'll be right behind you."

Ray Summers

10

R yan stirred, struggling to remember where he was, not wanting to open his eyes. It was a game he had played traipsing around Europe for eight years. This morning, it was easy. A mental glimmer of last night's near-arrest focused him on his location and purpose. He retrieved his watch from the nightstand and checked the time. There was no need to hurry. His first decision of the day was forgoing the morning swim. Yesterday morning, the motel pool had proven inadequate for serious lap swimming. A shower was the next important decision; there he would plan the rest of his day.

Breakfast with Bert Henderson was already on the program, a perfect opportunity to request that Jean Harris transcribe the taped statements for him. There were four of Banner's victims on tape now.

Ryan's second conversation with Marsha Horton had gone well. Marsha did not know the name of the inspector who had taken her into the search room, but she had a good eye for detail and was able to give a decent description of Banner. She also recalled the time and date of the incident. Her transcribed telephone statement would be faxed to the Customs Office of Enforcement in San Diego. Agents there would see that it was reviewed and signed by Marsha. The statement would then be returned to him by overnight special-delivery mail.

Ryan would take Lupe Martinez's statement to her as soon as it was in paper form. The older sister would sign as a witness, avoiding the mother's involvement – a deal he had made with Lupe. He planned to have Ted and Jill Cowden sign their transcribed statements as he headed back to D.C. via San Antonio. The Cowden parents would witness those documents.

Ryan turned off the shower and took a towel from the wall rack. He could be out of here by Monday or Tuesday if the *El Jefe* of Mexican Customs would show up at his office today and give the OK for an interview of the Mexican woman. That would leave only the angry lady he had followed to the RV park last night. She had admitted trouble with a Customs inspector. She had a story. He wanted it on paper and under oath. If she would just stop being angry long enough to listen to him, he was certain he could turn her around.

Ryan stepped out of the bathroom to the nearby clothing rack, removed a small notebook from his coat pocket and made a note to call the office in Albuquerque and advise the RAC there that the New Mexico woman had been found. He stepped to the nightstand, checked the time again and wondered if Miss New Mexico was an early riser.

He shaved and put on a light-blue shirt, dark-blue tie and the spare suit he had learned to always carry, this one a light gray. He would be going all Italian today, appearing out of place again in the land of boots, Levi's and guayabera shirts. Thinking this would be a one-day headquarters trip he had departed the training center with no casual clothing, only the extra back-up suit. The suit was a $600 Baroni Uomo. The $100 shirt and $50 tie bore Forzieri logos. He had found that quality clothing, while expensive, aside from giving favorable impressions, survived frequent and extended travel better than budget buys. The U.S. ambassador in Madrid had insisted that all attaches to the Embassy present favorable appearances at all times. Though no financial incentive had been offered, Ryan took him at his word.

He sat on the bed and slipped on the black Belvedere Italian shoes. Admittedly these $500 handmade ostrich and crocodile leather shoes were an extravagance, his favorite among all else in the extensive European wardrobe he had managed to acquire. The shoes were absolutely beautiful and very comfortable. He wouldn't mind at all appearing out of place again today, dressed in a small fortune.

The shoes could use a shine; he might risk a touch-up by one of the street kids in Acuña. That might salvage another visit across the border from being a complete loss. He tied his shoes and stood up.

The sheepskin pouch containing his Remington .45 semi-automatic was in the open briefcase. He tossed in a tablet of notes, file folders, the recorder and telephone attachment, closed the case and carried it out the door to the car. There was plenty of time for a run by the RV park. If it appeared anyone was stirring, he might have another go at Miss New Mexico.

He rounded the southeast corner of the motel and drove along the row of cars parked in front of the rooms. Near the front of the motel, he stopped suddenly, backed up and came to a stop behind a red Ranchero nosed into one of the parking slots near the motel restaurant. A glance downward at the New Mexico license plate confirmed that this was the Ranchero he had followed last night. He pulled into an open space nearby.

The breakfast buffet touted on the marquee was in full swing. Most of the crowd appeared to be businessmen and drivers of the now-half-dozen semis parked on the back lot. Ryan saw only four women, none of them the driver of the Ranchero. He started toward the registration desk then realized he didn't know whom to ask for. Last night, the deputies had refused to give up the woman's name or any details of what was happening. They promised full cooperation when Ryan could prove his interest was official. What else would it be? Why else would anyone be interested in such an unpleasant woman?

He returned to his car, backed to the rear of the Ranchero again, stopped and scrutinized the rooms. He tried not to speculate as to why she would be in a motel room this early in the morning instead of her motor home. Perhaps she wasn't unpleasant all the time. Probably could be nice-looking, even pretty if she cared to be. Perhaps just a little too thin, he had noticed yesterday at the Mexican Customs office. He was inclined to wait her out, but there were the tapes to be transcribed. He would catch angry woman later at her motor home. He drove to the highway and turned southward toward town, watching for the restaurant where he was to meet Henderson.

Betty's Ranch House was a large white-frame building on the west side of Avenue F, the highway street. The crowded parking lot contained two green National Park Service vans, a black-and-white Texas Department of Public Safety patrol car, a green-and-white Border Patrol van, and a blue-and-white city police cruiser. Henderson had mentioned that the owner of the cafe was a retired Del Rio police officer.

Inside, there was hardly a vacant stool along the black-topped counter that stretched from the right of the doorway to the rear of the dining room. Two National Park Rangers glanced up as he entered. Booths with padded seats lined the other three walls. Tables and chairs filled the space between the booths and the counter. Henderson motioned from across the room. Ryan made his way around several empty tables to the booth occupied by the resident agent in charge and a thin, middle-aged man with short, bristling white hair. "This is Greg Paulson," Henderson said. "He keeps our patrol boat running. Greg, this is Ryan Shaw."

Greg offered a slender, sun-browned hand that matched his face.

"Nice to meet you, Greg." They shook hands. Ryan glanced at two border patrolmen seated in the booth behind Henderson, then toward two highway patrolmen in a booth further down. The breakfast served at Betty's Ranch House must be fantastic. Ryan slid into the booth beside Paulson and immediately noticed a smirk on Henderson's face.

"Well, how did things turn out last night?" the RAC asked as the smirk grew.

"You mean at Tom's?"

"Afterward."

Ryan hesitated. The picture came to him. "The deputies called you?"

Henderson chuckled. "Carl wanted a little verification before turning you loose last night." He chuckled again. "I told him you were here on special assignment. He said that was all he needed to know." Henderson maintained eye contact, and the smirk.

The deputy must have mentioned the woman. The RAC's stare said he wanted to know more. Ryan looked away and shifted in his seat, wondering if the Del Rio Customs Agent's Office had even one secret from the rest of the world. "After I left Tom's last night, I saw a vehicle that looked like one I might be interested in – a Ranchero with New Mexico plates."

Henderson picked up his coffee and slowly sipped it without breaking his stare.

Ryan continued, "And a good-looking woman driving it."

"I know her," Paulson interrupted. "Fixed up a boat for her a couple of months back, a Boston Whaler with an old Johnson eighty-five. She's from Socorro, New Mexico, staying out at the S&S trailer park. Been here all summer, looking for her sister and brother-in-law." He looked at Henderson, "You know, the ones that disappeared on the lake the first part of summer."

"Oh, yeah," Henderson nodded. "I know her, too." He turned to Ryan. "She found out we had a boat, came to the office wanting someone to chauffeur her around the lake. She claimed the Park Service had searched the wrong area. I told her civilians weren't allowed on the patrol boat. She stormed out, very, very angry." Henderson made a face, took a sip of coffee, then said, "So what did you want with...." His mouth froze and his eyes slowly widened.

Henderson was an open book. Whatever was happening inside his head could be read on his face. He lowered his coffee cup. "Is she one of the women in Greene's memo? Banner took her into the search room?" His eyes continued to widen, like a kid opening a Christmas present.

Ryan didn't answer. He took a breath and exhaled it slowly as he looked for a waitress. He had worked with tight-lipped foreign intelligence officials for eight years. Open discussions of this investigation were wearing thin. He caught the waitress's eye and mouthed the word "coffee." She nodded.

Someone behind him yelled, "Hey, Denise, you found the Mayor yet?"

A stool at the counter squeaked as a slender black woman in National Park green swung around. "Not yet. Haven't even found his big boat." She folded her arms and stretched long legs out in front of her. "But we're still looking. A Mexican Coast Guard unit from Matamoros came in last night hauling a boat loaded with electronic underwater-search gear." She gazed around the room and spoke louder. "We're extending the search to include the Devil's River arm. Anyone with a boat that wants to help out, stop by the office."

"You won't find the mayor's boat over there," Greg Paulson shouted into Ryan's left ear. Ryan leaned forward as Paulson continued. "I know that boat. The mast is way too tall to pass under the highway bridge."

Ryan rubbed his ear, picturing the long bridge he had measured separating the Rio Grande and Devil's River portions of the lake.

"That's true." Denise turned her attention to Greg. "But, we have another one missing now, a college student from Amarillo, and he could be anywhere." She looked around the room. "He's twenty years old, had a red kayak and a green Volkswagen Bug with Texas plates. Anyone sees anything like that, give me a call, please." The stool squeaked again, announcing Denise's turn back toward the counter.

The Volkswagen registered immediately with Ryan. He looked across the table at Henderson, wondering if the RAC was aware that his agents had arranged for a green Volkswagen Bug to be towed from the lake area yesterday. Henderson sipped his coffee and said, "The mayor is history."

"Afraid so," Paulson agreed. "He never should have butted heads with that Mexico City bunch. No way he was going to stop them."

"Stop them?" Henderson shook his head and chuckled. "Come on, you know better than that. Trying to stop them was just public-image stuff. He wanted in. Casinos are sprouting up all over the area that was supposed to be a shoreline park." The RAC looked at Ryan. "It's turning into a little Las Vegas, and the former land owners, which includes the mayor, are pissed over being scammed out of their land and left out of the casino cash flow. That's what it's really all about."

Ryan nodded and looked away. He had heard this story yesterday from the Immigration officer in charge and it still held no interest to him. What happened to the coffee he'd ordered? And where was Tom Del Castillo this morning? Tom should be informed that search teams would soon be all over the location he had chosen for a machine-gun delivery point. When searchers learned of the impounded Volkswagen and where it had been parked, a mob would assemble and probably remain under the Pecos River Bridge. Ryan looked back across the table. He would let Henderson know about the Volkswagen as soon as they could speak in private. But first, he had business of his own. "I have some statements on tape that need transcribing. I would like Jean to help me with that if it's all right with you."

"Sure, anything to help out."

Ryan had a mental picture of Henderson hovering over Jean, waiting for her to type the statements out. It was either that or send the tapes to headquarters for transcribing. Headquarters was a zoo. Things disappeared there. Leaks to the press were common. Better to have Henderson's nose in everything than risk starting over from scratch or seeing the Cowden family on television.

Henderson and Greg were still on Mexican politics. Denise and the other park ranger stood up. Ryan watched them pay their check and leave. His thoughts turned to the missing people: the mayor of Acuña and his party of four, a college student, the New Mexico woman's sister and brother-in-law, all gone without a trace. Now that was pretty damn strange. He wondered if anyone else thought so.

A coffee mug appeared in front of him. The waitress filled it, poured refills for the others and took breakfast orders. She had auburn hair and a face full of freckles, like the New Mexico woman, but the waitress was heavier. Ryan thought about his unwilling potential witness. She had retrieved her confiscated pistol from Mexican customs and handled an unpleasant encounter with U.S. Customs Inspector Banner to her own satisfaction, apparently. Displeased with official efforts, she had acquired a boat and was conducting a private search for her missing sister and brother-in-law. Pretty spunky, Ryan thought, feeling more than a twinge of admiration for the angry woman from New Mexico.

Greg had worked on her boat, knew where she was from and where she was staying. What else did Greg know? Ryan was about to broach the subject, but the thought of Henderson's presence stopped him. He had seen enough of that man's sneer for one morning. Questions about the New Mexico woman would bring it back. More information on her would come soon enough. Maybe he would check the motel again after breakfast.

Ray Summers

11

Sarah noticed that the FBI agent wasn't drinking his coffee, nor was he writing much in the small notebook he had placed on the table in front of him. She also noticed that he seemed more interested in the plates of pancakes, toast, eggs, bacon, sausage, biscuits and fresh fruit coming from the motel's breakfast buffet than the fact that someone had tried to kill her yesterday.

"What about fingerprints?" she asked, bringing his attention back from the chow line. "There might be fingerprints on the fuel cans he filled with water."

"I'm sure the Sheriff's Office will be glad to check that for you, Miss Dobbs, and eventually match any prints found to those of the culprit or culprits who stole your..." he glanced down at the notebook, "...fifteen gallons of outboard gasoline."

Sarah felt her anger growing as he finished this condescending remark, but for the most part she remained in control. "I didn't call the FBI about three cans of gasoline, Mr. Kline. I called the FBI because someone arranged for me to be stranded on the lake yesterday. I don't know why. I don't know who it was, or what would have happened to me if I hadn't managed to escape. You keep asking me why anyone would want to do that. I don't know. I've told you everything I know. You're the one who is supposed to find out why. That's what the FBI does, isn't it? Investigate crimes committed on federal property, which I understand includes national parks and recreation areas. Is that correct? Do you investigate crimes committed on Lake Amistad or not?"

The FBI agent closed the little notebook and slipped it into his inside coat pocket. "Look, Miss Dobbs, there are a lot of people out on the lake now, searching for the missing mayor. Many of them are armed, out-of-uniform Mexican officials and I'm sure they might appear a little... menacing, to say the least, to..." He paused. Sarah knew he had stopped himself before saying "a woman." The agent continued, "...to someone alone and stranded." He took a deep breath and leaned forward.

Sarah knew what was coming next: This is not my jurisdiction; there's no evidence of a crime; we're short of funds, short of people, short of time. She had heard them all during the past two months. She decided not to listen this time, pushed her chair back and stood up.

Behind the FBI agent, another man in a business suit caught her eye. He was sitting three tables away. He looked up, nodded and smiled – the tall man with the strange green eyes. A Customs agent he had said last night, looking for a woman driving a Ranchero, wanting to know about the incident at the dam. A government official wanting something from her. That was a switch. She walked over to his table. "Exactly what is it you want, Mister?"

"Shaw, Ryan Shaw." He stood up and offered his hand.

Sarah was five feet ten inches tall. This agent Shaw was a good four inches taller, well-groomed this morning, in an expensive and stylish gray suit, blue tie, and no longer smelling of stale beer. She didn't shake hands.

"I didn't intend to interrupt anything." Ryan looked toward the FBI agent still seated at the other table.

"What do you want?"

"A statement from you about what happened the night the inspector took you into the search room."

"I didn't go into any room with him, just into the main building."

"Then I would like a statement about that."

"Why?"

"Because other women have gone into the search room with him."

So that was what it was about. Someone had complained. Sarah stared up into the fixed piercing blue green eyes. Their color seemed liquid, darkening and lightening as she watched. She heard the FBI agent clear his throat as he approached behind her.

"Miss Dobbs, I really must be going. The matter we were discussing is really not in my...."

"I don't want to hear it." Sarah turned to face him. "If you're not going to do anything, then just go."

"If I had any evidence of a violation...."

"The evidence just might be my dead body, Mr. Kline, and I just hope it washes up on the Mexican side of the lake where there's at least a small chance that something will be done about it."

The FBI agent raised his eyebrows and left without further comment. Sarah turned back to the tall Customs man.

"And exactly what happens to women who go into that little room?"

"I'd rather not say for now. Maybe after you tell me what happened to you."

"I don't have time for this." She turned to leave.

"Some were high-school girls," Ryan said quietly.

Sarah hesitated.

"I need your help," Ryan continued. "It will only take a few minutes of your time."

She turned and looked back. He lifted his metal briefcase with one arm and tapped on it with his other hand. "I have a tape recorder for taking your statement. It's noisy in here. We could go out to my car – or yours. It will only take a few minutes."

High school girls. The bastard was making kids take their clothes off? She should have at least filled out a form, made a complaint or something. "Let's go." She led the way to the door, noticing that she had taken the attention of everyone in the room away from their eggs and pancakes.

Outside, the bright sunlight struck her full in the face. She squinted, raised a forearm to shade her eyes, and hurried to the Ranchero two motel doors away. She unlocked the driver's door, opened it, slid under the wheel and cleared the passenger seat of her briefcase, jacket and straw hat. The Customs agent was waiting. She unlocked the other door and he slid in beside her. As she straightened in the seat, she saw that his wavy black hair nearly touched the top of the cab. He opened his briefcase and took out the cassette recorder. "I'm going to turn the recorder on, give the date, time, our names... by the way, what is your name?"

"Sarah Dobbs."

"Miss or Mrs.?"

"Miss. And before I say anything with a recorder going I want to know exactly what this is about, and where this recording is going to end up. I don't need a lawsuit on my hands."

"I'm investigating allegations of misconduct against one of our Customs inspectors. Your statement will be used as evidence to prove or disprove those allegations, depending on what you have to say."

Generic answer, she thought. When she made no comment, he continued.

"Now, Miss Dobbs, as I was about to say, just tell what happened after you arrived at the port of entry. When you're finished, I may have a few questions. This will be typed in affidavit form, and I'll bring it to you for your signature."

Sarah nodded. She was satisfied that she wasn't going to get any more out of him until he had his statement. He started the recorder, placed it on the dashboard, gave their identities and the date, and nodded in her direction.

"Two months ago..." Only two months ago, Sarah thought, not the two years it felt like to her. "I drove across the dam to the Mexican marina looking for a boat and a guide to help look for my sister and brother-in-law, who had disappeared on the lake. When I returned to the port of entry, the Customs inspector had me step out of my car while he searched it." He searched me, too, she thought, with his eyes... those, small dark, anxious eyes that had first alerted her. "Then he asked me to go inside the building with him. When we got there, he typed something into a computer terminal, waited for a reply, then said something to another inspector, a Hispanic man, who was sitting by the window drinking coffee. He was the only other person there. He got up and went outside after the blond inspector spoke to him." She remembered the feeling of uneasiness that had caused, but her mind had said she was being silly, that this was the United States, and these men were federal officers. The trapped feeling had not gone away. "The inspector who had asked me to come into the building said I matched the description of a drug smuggler from Carlsbad, New Mexico; plus I was driving a vehicle commonly used to smuggle drugs, so I would have to be searched. I said all right. Drugs are a problem everywhere, even in the small town where I live, Socorro, New Mexico, and I've read about women being used as couriers. I was willing to be searched. Then he informed me that there were no women inspectors available, and that I would either have to submit to a search by him or wait two hours for a female inspector to come from.... I didn't know the area then. I think he said Eagle Pass." She remembered that he had kept his eyes on the front window while telling her this, watching the other inspector outside.

When he did turn back to her, the darting black eyes had devoured her, missing no part of her body. She remembered backing away until the wall stopped her. "I told him that was ridiculous and asked him what he was trying to get away with." He had walked to a nearby door, opened it and turned on a light inside a small, closet-size room containing only a wooden bench. "He said I could go into the room, take my clothes off, hand them out for him to search, and that would be good enough. That was when I left." Ran, she should have said. She darted out from the building, got into the Ranchero, locked the doors and drove away. When no one came after her, she knew she had done the right thing. The thought of being undressed in that small room with that man anywhere around made her shudder even now.

Ryan leaned forward and clicked off the tape recorder. "I'm sorry that happened to you. This man has only been with the Customs Service for eighteen months. Someone made a mistake hiring him. We are in the process of correcting that mistake." He straightened in the seat, and his voice changed to a less somber tone. "I have a few questions, just the date and time if you can remember, and the physical descriptions of the two inspectors."

"What happened to the women who did go into the room?"

"There were four others that I know about: a fourteen-year-old, a seventeen-year-old and two women in their early twenties. One of the girls disrobed and was fondled. The other one refused to remove her clothing, but was fondled anyway. One woman stripped because she didn't want to get the teenage boy she was with into trouble. The other woman, I haven't talked to yet, but I know she was taken into the search room."

"All so young...." Sarah glanced up at the rearview mirror, glad that it was adjusted so she couldn't see herself. The pervert wouldn't try to search her now. That had been two months ago, before the weight loss, peeling skin and daily 12-hour blow-dries, back when she had a bust-line, a complexion and something besides wire for hair. She looked down at her chapped hands, broken nails, faded jeans and stained white sneakers. In her billowing, light-blue, long-sleeve shirt and down-turned straw hat, she must look like the scarecrow from "The Wizard of Oz." Alone, out on the lake for the past eight weeks, that was exactly how she had wanted to look, like a man. It hadn't bothered her before. Why was she even thinking about it now?

He pushed the cassette deck's record button again. "Do you remember the date and approximate time you arrived at the port of entry?

"Yes." Sarah stared at the motel door in front of the Ranchero. "It was Friday, July the first. Every fishing guide and boat on both sides of the border was booked for the long holiday weekend. I came back across around nine, just after dark."

"Describe the two men on duty at the port, please."

"The one who searched the Ranchero, then asked me into the building, was about my height: five-ten, medium build, blond hair, blond bushy mustache. His eyes were dark, black, I think, close together and small."

"How old?"

"Thirty, I guess."

"The other man?"

"Hispanic, about forty-five or fifty." She thought for a moment. "That's all I remember about him."

The recorder was turned off. "That's about it. I'm not sure when this will be ready. Will you be at the RV park for a few more days?"

She would never spend another night in that park. She had thought about it. She would only be in town two more days. "I'll be in town until Friday, but I'll be staying at the Holiday Inn." She nodded over her right shoulder, toward another motel on the far side of a vacant block.

The agent looked in that direction, then back at her, a puzzled look on his face.

"It's a long story." She pulled one of the business cards from her shirt pocket and handed it to him. "My Socorro telephone number. The one here won't be good after Friday."

"Your sister and brother-in-law still haven't been found?"

"No. They've been gone almost three months now."

"Bad weather?"

"No, clear and sunny weeks before and weeks afterward. Nothing to do with the weather."

"What's the problem here? Why do people keep disappearing on this lake?"

"You mean the mayor and his party?"

"Yes, and now there's another one, a college kid in a kayak. I just heard about it this morning."

Sarah felt the color drain from her face. She had seen this young man Saturday morning as she launched the Boston Whaler. He was carrying the red kayak down the old highway right-of-way across the lake from the ramp. Now he was missing? Like Laura and Mike, like the mayor's party, like she almost was.

"Mr. Shaw, would you mind going out to the RV park with me? I have to pick up a few things, and I'd rather not go back there alone."

For a moment, the agent had another puzzled look on his face, and then he smiled. "Be glad to, as long as I'm not getting into an angry-husband or -boyfriend situation."

She managed a smile back. "No, no husband or boyfriend. I'll explain it all to you on the way. And could we take your car, please?"

Ray Summers

12

Jean Harris looked up from her desk as Ryan closed the door behind him. "Good morning," she said.

Ryan returned her greeting, glancing toward the drone of voices coming from the squad room at the end of the hall. As he drove up he had seen a sheriff's patrol car, a Park Service van, and three plain sedans parked at the rear of the building. "Big meeting?" he asked.

Jean shrugged. "Guess so. They just started showing up a few minutes ago."

Ryan removed a cassette from his briefcase and placed it on her desk. "There's four statements on the tape that need to be transcribed, please." he said. "I checked with Bert about asking you to do that, but if you're busy on something else, I can send them out."

"No problem. Something interesting, I hope." She cocked her head sideways, smiling.

"I believe the subject of these statements is known locally as 'Magic Fingers.'"

Well...." She seemed pleased. "I think I'll just get right on these." Jean stood up and stepped into a nearby storage room.

"Just rough drafts," Ryan said toward the open door. "I need to do a little editing, then you can put them in affidavit form."

She came back out with a desk-size cassette machine, foot pedal and headset. "Rough drafts won't take long." She sat down and began connecting wires. Ryan picked up his briefcase and walked down the hall toward the squad room.

Carl, the deputy, Park Ranger Denise, Tom Del Castillo, Henderson and the man Sarah had identified as an FBI agent were seated around a long gray table in the middle of the room. Each one of them had a cup of coffee. Ryan opened the door to his borrowed office and slipped inside without interrupting. He suspected the gathering had something to do with the green Volkswagen. Henderson had been visibly upset when Ryan told him about it.

A note-pad on the borrowed office desk had the phone number for the Albuquerque office. Ryan picked up the phone and punched in the number. The agent he previously spoke with answered. He told him to disregard the search for the owner of the Ford Ranchero. "I found her here, thanks." He hung up.

He had found her all right, but didn't quite know what to think of her. Trying to search Lake Amistad alone seemed absurd but he certainly could understand it. Given the same circumstances, he would do the same. He admired her courage and tenacity. Someone putting water in her fuel tanks and stalking her was a little bizarre. He was inclined to agree with the FBI about that. Weeks alone on the lake and then more people disappearing could stimulate anyone's imagination. Ryan considered that for a moment. His own imagination could be energized by that many disappearing people if he cared to think about it.

The space between the bottom of the office door and the thin commercial carpeting made it difficult not to listen to the proceedings taking place in the squad room.

"I'll have the Volkswagen moved to our covered parking area," the deputy said. "We'll do a print search and keep it there until I hear from someone."

"Good," Denise said. "I would like to have some of your people at the bridge when we look that area over."

"Two on the way there now," Carl answered.

"Sorry, Tom," Denise said, "but we need to move on this."

"No problem. We're done up there."

The FBI agent spoke. "Customs had the car moved from under the Pecos Bridge north of Comstock?" The voice and probably the look asked why.

"We were watching the place for a boatload of parrots," Tom covered, wanting to keep the gun operation confidential. "The car might have scared our smugglers away, so I had the Sheriff's Office tow it."

"Did you get any parrots?" The FBI agent sounded skeptical. There was a ripple of laughter.

"No, probably too much activity with everyone searching for the mayor."

"Going to be a lot more," Denise said. "I'm moving everybody up there to look for this boy. His name is Dean Patterson. Here's copies of his driver's license photo. His folks are in town, drove in from Amarillo last night. I met with them, and the father is a retired Amarillo policeman. He'll probably want to see the car when he hears that we've got it."

"Any objections from the FBI?" the deputy asked.

"None. We're out of it unless there is some indication of foul play in the park area."

"Then I'll give the Pattersons a call," Carl said. "Where are they staying, Denise?"

"Best Western."

Ryan moved the note-pad in front of him, picked up a pen and wrote the name Patterson on the bottom of the page.

The meeting broke up. The rear door opened and closed several times, car engines came to life outside. Tom and the RAC were chuckling as they passed by the office door.

Ryan pulled a small notebook from his shirt pocket, found a number he had written less than an hour ago, picked up the phone and called the Holiday Inn.

"Room 225, please," he said in a low voice, staring at the open space below the door. He should be across the river now finding out if he had permission to interview the Mexican woman.

"Hello."

"Sarah, this is Ryan. The parents of the missing college student are here in town. Their name is Patterson. They're staying at the Best Western. I'm sure they will talk to you if you explain your situation."

Ryan hung up before Sarah could reply. It appeared they were on a first-name basis now. She looked thoughtful and put the phone down. The missing college student's parents were in town... and might talk to her? She was sitting on the bed, phone directory in her lap. She had been trying to find someone to help retrieve her boat she had beached and abandoned last night. Paulson, the man who had put the Boston Whaler back in shape for her, wasn't answering at his shop. Park rangers and sheriff's deputies were occupied with the search. She had decided to go to the marina boat ramp with a can of fuel and hope for a ride with a departing search team. Then the Customs agent had called. Why would she want to talk to the missing boy's parents? She looked across the room at the drawn window drapes.

Patterson, the agent said their name was. What did she have to ask them? "Mr. and Mrs. Patterson, my name is Sarah Dobbs. My sister and brother-in-law disappeared on the lake two months ago. I wonder if you could somehow help me find out what happened to them. They were looking for ancient pictographs. What was your son doing?" Sarah stared silently for a moment. Perhaps it would be useful to know why their boy was out on the lake alone. She stood up, gathered her straw hat and briefcase from the bed and walked to the door. The Best Western was ten or twelve blocks back toward town. She could check service stations along the way for a loaner gas can to take fuel out to the stranded boat.

♦　　♦　　♦

"The room number for the Pattersons, please." Sarah managed a smile for the young Hispanic man behind the counter.

"One twenty-six."

"Thank you." Sarah moved to a house phone at the end of the counter and picked it up.

"They aren't in," a feminine voice said behind her.

Sarah turned. A small young blonde woman smiled at her.

"I heard you ask for the Pattersons. They left a few minutes ago. I'm not sure when they will be back. Did you want to see them about Dean? Do you have some news?" The girl looked hopeful.

"Dean?"

"My fiancé, Dean Patterson – he's missing. Do you have some news?"

"No." Sarah shook her head and replaced the telephone headset in its cradle. "I only wanted to ask a few questions about... Dean. My sister and her husband are also missing. I thought we might compare notes."

"Oh." The girl slumped.

"Sorry," Sarah said. The girl turned away, hesitated and looked back. "I'm sorry to hear about your sister and her husband. I was here with Dean until Friday. Maybe I can be of some help."

13

The terrain northwest of Ciudad Acuña was flat and, except for an occasional small homestead clearing contained nothing but mesquite, greasewood and cenizo. At nine in the morning, traffic was practically nonexistent on the two-lane highway. Ryan covered the twelve miles in less than fifteen minutes. The road curved gradually to the right, and the waters of Lake Amistad appeared on the left. Two adobe buildings crowded the left lane of the blacktop at the Mexican end of Amistad Dam. Ryan pulled across the highway and parked between the buildings.

Two Mexican officers lounged on a tattered sofa near the end of the porch of the building nearest the dam. Ryan recognized the Customs uniforms. The men remained seated as Ryan approached. He stepped onto the porch, presented his credentials and spoke to the two Customs inspectors in Spanish. "United States Customs. I have permission from Comandante Espejo to speak with a woman who works here."

Eyes widened in surprise, not an unusual reaction from other native speakers to Ryan's native Sonoran Spanish. Before either could reply, a small, narrow-faced man in a collapsed garrison hat and wrinkled olive-drab uniform stepped from a nearby doorway. Ryan noticed a single silver bar on each shoulder epaulet. He handed the lieutenant the letter from the Distrito Comandante de Aduana granting permission to interview Elvia Arispe-Lorenzo. The lieutenant began shaking his head as he studied the document, then asked the seated men. "The woman Elvia who works for Immigration, her name is Lorenzo, no?"

"*Si*," the younger of the two men answered.

The lieutenant turned to Ryan. "This woman works for Immigration." He motioned toward the other building.

Ryan frowned. Green's memorandum said the woman cooked and kept house for Mexican Customs. Apparently, that was a mistake. He reached for the letter.

The lieutenant waved the letter in front of him in a fanning motion. "Come, I will introduce you." The officer stepped off the porch and marched toward the other building. Ryan followed.

The furnishings on the other porch were covered with faded serapes. Two automobile bench seats, Ryan guessed. He followed the lieutenant through an open door. A large, dark man in sage green uniform sat alone at the far end of a long wooden dining table, coffee and breakfast before him. He did not appear happy at the intrusion.

"A U.S. Customs officer," the lieutenant announced. "He wishes to speak with the woman, Elvia Lorenzo. Is she here?"

The seated man glared.

"My name is Ryan Shaw." Ryan moved near enough to offer his hand. "I was told that Señorita Lorenzo worked for Customs, so I obtained permission from the Distrito Comandante de Aduana to speak to her."

Eyes fixed on the other officer, the seated man ignored Ryan and his outstretched hand. The lieutenant stepped to a nearby doorway and shouted the woman's name. The large man erupted from the table. "¡Cabron!" he shouted. "Get out." He moved to the smaller man, towering over him. "Do not shout at my people. Go!" He pointed toward the door and turned to Ryan. "You have no authority here. Permission from this *cabron's jefe* means nothing to me. Get out."

Ryan followed the Customs lieutenant through the door. Personal feud? Turf war? Something was going on between these two, something that might be exploited into useful information... but that would take time and effort... and he was no longer in that business and this wasn't his turf. Alone, he may have talked his way into a quick interview. But there was no salvaging the situation with the Immigration officer's enemy at your side. The Mexican Customs lieutenant had used him in a frontal assault.

Safely back on the other porch, the troublemaker handed back the letter. Ryan waved away the apologies, managed a *"Grácias"* and departed. Instead of crossing the dam and driving back on the U.S. side as he had intended, Ryan retraced his route back to Ciudad Acuña and the main port of entry.

The Mexican Immigration officer on duty at the main port of entry listened patiently to Ryan's story, jotted down a few notes and said he would inform *El Jefe*, who would not be back until tomorrow. Ryan thanked him and drove north across the bridge, remembering a time when Mexican officials would turn a border town upside down for a U.S. Customs agent.

At the Del Rio port of entry, a Customs inspector with a shaggy blond mustache greeted him. "Please state your citizenship."

"U.S.," Ryan replied. The women's descriptions of Chuck Banner had been right on.

"Bringing anything from Mexico?"

"Nothing."

"Thank you." Banner leaned nearer the open passenger's window. "And when we get around to having our little chat, I want my attorney and union rep present."

Ryan had given little thought to the "chat" Banner was referring to, knowing only that it would not occur before evidence warranting Banner's dismissal or resignation was in hand. Now staring into the dark, piglike eyes, Ryan realized there would be no resignation. Banner had tied up ATF supervisors with grievance and civil-suit proceedings to avoid being dumped. His intent to repeat that stratagem was now perfectly clear. "Magic Fingers" would not be frightened or shamed into quiet submission. He would go down kicking and screaming. Perhaps, Ryan thought, it was time to start thinking about his own strategy.

Banner looked away, straightened up from the window and turned toward the next car in line. Ryan drove on through the port, crossed the loop road, parked in front of the Customs agent's office and went inside. Jean looked up from her desk. "The drafts are ready."

"Great," Ryan said as he strode down the hallway. "I'll be right back." Noting that the squad room was empty, he entered his borrowed office, picked up the telephone and punched in numbers for the commissioner's office in D.C. When an aide came on the line, Ryan identified himself and said, "I want someone from IA down here right away, an expert on personnel regs and the national agreement between Customs and the employee's union." Banner wasn't going to walk because of some technicality.

14

Jean Harris cranked out finished statements faster than Ryan could edit first drafts. He was down to the last one, which was Sarah's. It set him wondering how she had made out with the missing college student's parents. He didn't know why the mysterious disappearances had begun to nag him.

He pushed Sarah's statement aside and reached for the Del Rio telephone directory. The Yellow Pages had one local newspaper listed. He punched in the number. A woman's voice answered, "*Del Rio News-Herald.*" Ryan requested the archives section. The feminine voice informed him there was no such department. "We have microfiche available going back to 1954. If you have an approximate date I can pull the film, but you'll have to make an appointment and conduct your own search." The offer was not an enthusiastic one.

"You have no way to research subject matter?"

"No, we don't have the staff for that."

Ryan thanked her and hung up. The Park Service and Sheriff's Office would have records of lake mishaps, drownings and disappearances. He was still thinking about it when a sharp rap at the office door interrupted his thoughts.

Jean entered and dropped freshly typed pages onto his desk. "Marsha Horton," she said. "Now there's a real lovely."

"Looking out for young Mark." Ryan smiled. "Loyal and protective." He pulled the top page from the papers Jean had delivered. He had quickly learned that Jean Harris made no typing errors. He was checking his own dictated instructions to be sent along with Marsha Horton's affidavit. It took only a moment. Satisfied, he returned it to the other finished pages and handed them back to Jean. "Fax the whole thing to San Diego, please, and wait just a minute, this is the last draft."

He gathered Sarah's statement in front of him and quickly went over the last part, where Sarah refused to go into the search room. Ryan shook his head. She was tough but not to the degree she pretended. News of the missing college student had visibly shaken her. Parking the Ranchero at one motel and staying at another made it clear that she was frightened. It also demonstrated that she was not stupid. Ryan finished editing Sarah's statement, crossing out his comments on her descriptions of the inspectors. He handed the statement to Jean. As she closed the door behind her, Ryan turned back to the telephone directory. He quickly found what he was looking for and jotted down the address of the Val Verde County Library.

♦   ♦   ♦

Sitting in the front passenger seat beside Ryan, Lupe Martinez read her statement. When she looked up, Ryan asked if there was anything she cared to add or change. She shook her head. "Raise your right hand," he said in a somber tone. "Do you swear that this statement is the truth, the whole truth and nothing but the truth, so help you God?"

"Yes, sir."

Ryan handed her his pen. Using the silver metal Halliburton briefcase between them for a desk, Lupe signed the document. "Thank you," Ryan said, retrieving papers and pen. "Now, how about bringing me another cup of coffee?" He had left Lupe's sister's house less than fifteen minutes earlier. Her signature as a witness was on the line below Lupe's. The first affidavit was complete.

Lupe returned with a Styrofoam cup of coffee, handed it to Ryan and removed the serving tray from the car window. Ryan thanked her again, put the window up and backed away from Nina's Drive-in. He drove slowly toward the old downtown area, watching for a sign Lupe's sister had described. It appeared outside the passenger window as he stopped for a traffic light. It read: Val Verde County Library, with an arrow at the bottom of the sign pointed to the right. He turned onto the quiet tree-lined residential street.

A large one-story brick building occupied the center of the third block on his left. It appeared well cared for and appreciated by the community, the kind of library that would accumulate newspaper and magazine clippings of local events, people and tourist attractions such as Lake Amistad.

♦ ♦ ♦

It was almost dark when Ryan arrived at the Ramada. Four eighteen-wheelers had already stopped for the night, backed against the wooden fence bordering the far end of the spacious rear parking area. Alone, in the center of the lot, trailer and boat attached, sat the red Ford Ranchero. Ryan parked near his room and looked across the vacant, treeless darkness on his left. The brightly lit Holiday Inn was a block away. He got out of the car, went directly to his room, called the other motel and asked the desk clerk to ring Sarah's room.

She answered on the first ring. After identifying himself, he said, "Your statement is ready. I can meet you in the lobby if you want to take care of it tonight."

"Is that where you are?"

"No, I'm across the vacant lot at the Ramada."

"Pick me up out front."

"Be there in two minutes."

When he pulled up, she was waiting in the lighted area in front of the office, dressed in jeans, white short-sleeve blouse and blue sneakers. Her hair seemed shinier. The jeans were new... and tight, nothing like the loose square-cuts he'd seen her in before. A light, pleasant smell came into the car with her.

"Head north," she said, closing the door. "I'll introduce you to the best T-bone this side of Albuquerque. You haven't eaten, have you?

No, and that steak sounds pretty good." Lunch had been a lukewarm taco at a convenience store near the port. He turned onto the highway, feeling her eyes on him as he accelerated to highway speed.

"I appreciate the call about the Pattersons," she said pleasantly as she leaned back and fastened her seat belt. "The parents were out but I

113

talked to the fiancé."

"Find out anything?"

"Found out everything." She settled into the seat, hands in her lap. "Dean Patterson and his girlfriend were doing a little treasure hunting."

"On the lake?"

"That's right. They were camped under the highway bridge just north of the Pecos boat ramp. The girl left a few days ago to visit her parents before classes started. She's feeling guilty about leaving."

"What were they looking for?" He noticed Sarah hesitate before answering, as if she had sensed something odd about his question or the tone of his voice.

"A gold mine," she finally said. "What else?" She shrugged. She squinted, studying his occasional glances and interested expression as best she could in the dimness and flashes from oncoming headlights.

Sarah continued, "It seems some relatives of the Patterson kid came across an old file cabinet somewhere belonging to a great-uncle who was something of a treasure hunter. He belonged to an organization or club of some kind that researched legends and stories of lost treasure. For a price, they provided researched information on any lost treasure or mine to club members that came with guarantees assuring that, number one, the treasure was real, and number two, that it had not been found." Sarah paused sensing that Ryan had become aware of her appraising stare she focused on the road ahead.

"What else?" Ryan prompted

"Curious about his treasure-hunting uncle, the boy learned from the discovered documents that the great-uncle was here in the Del Rio area to search for a lost gold mine called the Caracol, and then the old uncle mysteriously disappeared." Sarah inhaled deeply. "Never found him. That was two years ago."

She shrugged. "I was born and raised in New Mexico. Lost-mine and buried-treasure stories are nothing new to me. This time there's no map, no cryptic description or deathbed instructions but there is, for a change, an old rusty filing cabinet." She paused for a deep breath.

The Caracol mine name piqued Ryan's interest; same one Jimmy Del Castillo mentioned. Ryan alternated his attention between her and the empty road ahead. She was slowly shaking her head in doubt.

"So they had directions for locating the mine?" Ryan asked. He straightened in his seat, catching a glimpse of the puzzled look as it appeared on Sarah's face.

"Not exactly. According to the girl, the mine was likely to be located within walking distance of a railroad tunnel south of the confluence of the Pecos and Rio Grande."

"I'm familiar with that area," she continued. "It's the cove where my sister's cap was found and where I saw the mayor's sailboat Sunday afternoon, about two miles south of the tunnel. I've been thinking about that all day, since talking to...."

Ryan interrupted. "I read a story about an old man who disappeared two years ago. That must have been the Patterson boy's great-uncle. Have you heard about it?"

Sarah shook her head to say no. "Did he go missing on the lake?"

"Maybe, no one is sure. But he had been camping near the lake. Then his pickup and camper turned up in Mexico, abandoned on the highway south of Ciudad Acuña."

"I did hear some talk about that during the search for Laura and Mike, but that man didn't disappear on the lake. He didn't even have a boat."

"Do you know what he was doing here?"

"No."

"He was a treasure hunter." Ryan let that sink in for a moment. "Quite a successful one, too. According to a newspaper article on his disappearance, a scrapbook found in his camper contained newspaper clippings about his recovery of old bank and stagecoach robbery loot in New Mexico and Arizona. Also found among his belongings was a document indicating that a gold mine known as the Lost Caracol had been certified as genuine and still undiscovered by the treasure-research organization he belonged to, probably the same as where little Jimmy and Tom Del Castillo found their mine report, he thought. "The article I read gave no information for the mine's location, not even a state."

"What article? Where did you see anything like that?" She was beginning to sound angry again.

"The county library," Ryan said. "They have quite a file on Lake Amistad. After reading about the treasure hunter's disappearance, I dropped by the Sheriff's Office and talked to one of your buddies from last night, the small one. He said the old man was never found, only his pickup and camper on the outskirts of Ciudad Acuña. He said the man had camped near the Pecos River Bridge for two or three weeks before disappearing. Sheriff's deputies and Border Patrol had checked him out several times."

"You were checking the library for information about missing people?"

Ryan shrugged. "I knew about the mayor and his party. I heard about your situation at breakfast this morning just before I heard about the missing college student. After our little discussion this morning, I got a little curious. Still am."

"Who mentioned my situation this morning? Was I the breakfast topic?"

"Sort of. Your deputy pals called the local agent in charge last night to check me out and he brought the subject up. Craig Paulson was there and explained that you had been here all summer searching for your sister and brother-in-law. That's all there was to it, but yeah, I guess you could say you were the breakfast topic. Now tell me about the Patterson boy."

There was a long silence before she spoke. "The girl said Dean Patterson was very interested in history and had taken some geology classes in college. Among his great-uncle's files was a copy of a letter found in the University of Texas archives from a railroad worker who was employed as a hunter to keep the work camps supplied with fresh meat. The letter recounted how, one day, the hunter took two of the Chinese laborers from the tunneling crew with him downriver to retrieve a bear he had shot that fell into a deep crevasse. The laborers also found the a few small nuggets of gold and some black fossilized snails in the crevasse." Sarah paused.

"Zentner's steak house is about another mile, on the left...." she interjected. "Apparently the letter had enough details for the Lost Caracol Mine legend to be certified as genuine even though it didn't name the rivers."

"That's incredible," Ryan said. Her mention of the fossilized snails brought to mind again little Jimmy Del Castillo, which made him smile

"I know – another bizarre treasure story," Sarah added. "And this isn't even mining country. Everything around here is sediment and limestone. I'm no geologist but my ex-husband was and I have done some reading. Seams of gold could possibly have shifted down this way during Ice Age." She paused again.

"Dean's fiancé said he was reading a news article about the dam and the lake filling up, and how some of its geological features would be flooded. It mentioned the fossilized snails and the old railroad tunnel. He figured it was where the Lost Caracol Mine was located."

Static crackled from the walkie-talkie on the seat between them. Sarah glanced down. The radio had been silent since Ryan left the office. He had forgotten about it. The static came in short, sporadic bursts. Scrambled voice transmissions, probably Tom and the ATF team. Ryan had learned the smuggled machine-guns case was going down tonight at an alternate location. Tom was prepared for the sudden change in plans to a new delivery spot. He's a good man, Ryan thought as he turned the radio off.

"There's the steak house." Sarah pointed toward a green neon sign ahead on the left.

"I'm starving," Ryan said. "But, if you can wait a few minutes, there's someone I want you to meet.... Have you ever seen a petrified snail?" He waited for her response. None came. He glanced over. She was staring ahead, forehead wrinkled.

"That's what Patterson and his girlfriend were looking for," she said softly. "Petrified snails. They were supposed to be a marker for the mine."

"Do you know what the Spanish word is for snail?" Ryan asked.

"No, I don't know that."

"Caracol." Ryan replied. He kept driving a bit farther, then turned off the highway and drove between the stone pillars at the entrance to Laguna Verde Estates.

♦ ♦ ♦

Isabel Del Castillo didn't seem surprised to see him, nor did she hesitate after hearing his request. Jimmy was sent running for his treasure file and petrified snails. Isabel reminded Ryan of agents' wives in Nogales years ago. Nothing had ever surprised them either. Ryan declined a second invitation into the house, explaining that he and his friend in the car were on their way to dinner.

Jimmy returned and followed him to the car. Sarah pushed her door open.

"Jimmy, this is a friend of mine, Sarah Dobbs. She's spent a lot of time around the lake but never has seen a petrified snail." He turned to Sarah. "Sarah, I would like you to meet a good pal of mine, Jimmy Del Castillo."

"Hi, Jimmy."

"Ramshorn snails," Jimmy said. "They're from the Cretaceous period, sixty-six to a hundred forty-four million years ago." He handed the box to Sarah.

"Exactly where did you find them?" Ryan asked.

"Hmmm...." Jimmy frowned. "I don't remember. It was a long time ago, last year, maybe."

"On the Rio Grande side of the lake?" Sarah asked, lifting a snail to the car's dome light.

"Oh, yeah. We never come to the Devil's River side. I found the snails the same day we walked through the tunnel. There were bats in there." Jimmy's eyes widened. "Lots of them, all over the ceiling. Some of them had babies on their backs."

"Found the snails near the tunnel?" Ryan asked, as if he knew where the tunnel was.

"No, it was south of there, on the Mexican side. We were looking for the Lost Caracol gold mine."

"And you walked through the tunnel that day?" Sarah asked, replacing the snail and lifting a pale-yellow arrowhead from the box.

"Yeah, the lake was really low. That's another reason we went, to look for fishing plugs hung up on the brush. We found fifty-three. Want to see them?"

"No, not just now... thanks anyway." Sarah put the arrowhead back and handed Jimmy the box. "Do you think the water would be over the snails now that the lake is full?"

"Over the loose ones for sure, where I got these, but there was a whole cliff full of them, as tall as my house." He looked up into the dark, toward the roof of the two-story house. "I don't think the water would get that high."

"Thanks Jimmy." Ryan patted him on the back. "It's getting late. We have to run now. Can I borrow your file and get it back to you in a few days?"

"Sure," he answered. "Nice to meet you, Miss Dobbs."

"Nice to meet you, too, Jimmy."

Ryan handed the file to Sarah and walked around the car. He watched until Jimmy was back in the house before he got in and they headed for the steakhouse.

Ray Summers

15

They ordered two medium-well T-bone dinners, a glass of white wine for her and a bottle of Bohemia for him. Sarah opened the file and started to read the report on the lost gold mine.

"Tell me what it says," Ryan said.

Sarah grimaced and glanced around. The tables nearest them were empty; still, she spoke so softly that Ryan could hardly hear the words as she skimmed the pages. "Silas Jones is the name of the hunter who wrote the letter about the bear hunt and finding the mine. The report says he wrote every few days to his fiancée. He was working on the railroad to earn enough money for them to buy a farm after they married."

She ran her index finger over lines in the report. "He married her and bought a farm in the Texas Hill Country. He died young, not much long after, never made it back to look for the mine. After she passed away, her husband's letters found their way to an archive at the University of Texas. They sat there, unexamined for decades."

Sarah shook her head and turned a page, skimming the report further. "The Lost Caracol Mine also made its way into spoken legend from members of the crew of railroad workers who remembered Jones bringing back the gold nuggets from his hunt. The crew completed its work soon after and moved on to the next tunnel. Some of them talked about maybe someday going back to find the mine and more gold. It became a talked-about legend along the railroad line – near a tunnel not far from where two rivers met, somewhere in Texas."

Sarah looked up at Ryan. "You keeping up with this?" The agent sensed a pattern emerging that maybe explained why these people had disappeared.

"So get this," she alerted Ryan. "The mine was just talk until 1958, when an author researching the history of Texas railroads came across the Silas Jones letters. He quoted the one about the mine in his book."

Sarah read on and then looked up, a thoughtful expression on her face. "The crew working on the tunnel lived in a large cave near the confluence of the Pecos and Rio Grande. It was called Painted Cave back then because it contained so many pictographs. Now it's known as Parida Cave."

She briefly paused as a sad look came over her face. Sarah's voice choked a bit as she explained, "That's a place where my sister and brother-in-law wanted to take pictures for their cave-art book." Ryan finished the last of his beer and looked at her.

The waitress arrived with two large platters. Ryan ordered another Bohemia and white wine. When the waitress was out of earshot, Sarah leaned forward and whispered, "I've read about and listened to dozens of lost treasure tales. I never dreamed the day would come when I might take one seriously. But this report seems to corroborate everything."

"I'm from the border country in Arizona and I've heard my share of treasure stories, too," Ryan noted. "Like you said, this isn't gold country, but if I were a treasure hunter, I'd be on the lake early in the morning looking for petrified snails."

"Maybe you've spent too much time with little Jimmy. What's my excuse?" She laughed, cut a piece of steak and put it into her mouth. "The first thing I've eaten all day," she mumbled as she raked foil off from her baked potato.

Ryan cut into his steak and tried an oversized sample: tender, juicy and delicious. "So we have the old treasure hunter disappearing two years ago, your sister and brother-in-law, the treasure hunter's college student great-nephew just this week, and the mayor and his sailboat party. All vanished without a trace from the same relatively small area."

"I almost disappeared, too," Sarah said without looking up. "I'll never go out there alone again."

"I'm glad to hear that," Ryan said. "The part about not going back alone. All of this has a familiar ring to it, reminds me of a crazy old man that lived on his mining claim west of Nogales. He threatened people for years, accused everyone coming near his place of being claim jumpers. He finally shot and killed two deer hunters. He was arrested, found insane and sent to an asylum. His 'silver mine' was a small vein of quartz with streaks of lead in it." Ryan ended the story with a sip of beer.

Sarah had listened intently. "I've heard similar stories. You think that's what's happening here? A crazy person?"

"I think it's something to consider. The organization that researched the Caracol mine certified it authentic, so there are people who believe it exists. If one of them happens to be nuts...." He shrugged. "Filling gas cans with water and stalking someone with a rifle sounds pretty crazy to me. I'm glad to hear you're not planning on going back, and if you do, at least not alone." Ryan didn't look up from his steak.

Sarah was quiet for a moment, and then said. "So you do believe someone was stalking me?"

"Yes."

"But Laura and Mike weren't looking for treasure," Sarah noted.

"Could be a case of wrong place, wrong time with them. Maybe they were looking for more pictographs in the cove."

"Sounds possible. And the mayor and his friends sure didn't look like they were searching for gold," Sarah added.

"Might be something else entirely going on there," said Ryan.

They ate in silence for a while before Sarah said, "Laura's cap was found in the same cove where I saw the sailboat. If there is a crazy person guarding a lost mine, that's where he would be." She sipped from the wine glass and frowned. "But I've been all around that cove, walked it out. I spent over a week there after Laura's cap was found. I wasn't looking for a mine or petrified snails, but there certainly isn't anything around there for a bear to fall into, and no crazy...." She didn't finish.

Sarah was quiet for a moment, and then said. "So you do believe someone was stalking me?"

"Yes."

"You didn't believe it this morning."

"No, but I do now. You should go on home, back to New Mexico."

They stared at each other for a moment before Sarah spoke. "I was the only one still looking. Now they will look for the mayor and the

Patterson boy for a few more days, then the search will wind down, just like before. If I showed them this file and maybe something that... that appeared to be a mine, maybe they would look for a murderer instead of missing people." Sarah stared across the room, apparently lost in thought.

"Didn't I hear you say you were never going back on the lake alone?"

She blinked herself back from wherever she had gone, looked at him, raised her glass and sipped. "Monday morning, I have a date with the IRS at the federal courthouse in Albuquerque. A last chance to save my gift shop in Socorro. That means leaving here no later than Saturday. Tomorrow and Friday are all I have left." Sarah dabbed her eyes with a napkin. "I'll get an early start in the morning, go to the boat ramp and offer my boat to the search teams provided they take me along. That way I'll have at least a park ranger or deputy with me."

"You won't be able to look where you want."

Sarah dabbed her eyes again and forced a smile. "Well, that's the best I can do."

Ryan took another bite of dry steak and looked away. He had no time for what he was about to suggest. There were a hundred reasons why he should just get her signature on the statement and leave her to her own problems, but that would be ignoring the feeling that had tugged at him since their morning visit, a feeling he now sensed might be mutual.

He turned back to her and said, "When you sign your statement tonight, I'll be all caught up. Nothing to do tomorrow but check across the river about another interview." He inhaled and raised his eyebrows. "I'm pretty sure that won't take long, then we can ask Jimmy's father where they found the snails and go from there, that is, if you would like to go ahead and invite me to see the lake."

"You're offering to go with me tomorrow?"

"Sure. I always wanted to find a gold mine." He smiled.

"I'll have the boat ready by the time you finish your errand."

Ryan nodded. "I'll ask Jimmy's dad to loan us a rifle."

16

The sullen Mexican officer in the sage-green uniform told Ryan that *El Jefe* would not be in before noon. It was what Ryan had expected. He thanked the Mexican Immigration officer, left the office and boarded the northbound bus back across the bridge.

He was inclined to forget about the Mexican woman. He had statements from four victims. What could one more possibly add to the picture? Probably not much, but leaving unturned stones was against his nature. He would be back tomorrow. If El Jefe was still not available, the commissioner might arrange a little pressure from Mexico City.

The bus stopped at the U.S. port of entry. Ryan stepped off, was waved on by the Customs inspector and crossed the street toward the agents' office. He glanced at his watch. It was almost nine. His meeting with Sarah was at Paulson's boat shop north of town at 9:30. He should check in at the office again and let Jean know that he would be out for the rest of the day. He stepped around a dark-blue Corvette parked beside his own car and entered the building.

A young, thick-bodied Latino in a dark brown suit stood in front of Jean's desk. He shifted a steaming coffee mug to his left hand. "Fred Ochoa, Internal Affairs, Houston," he said and thrust his right hand toward Ryan. The requested IA assistance had arrived.

"Ryan Shaw." He shook Ochoa's hand and thought of the strange car out front. "Your Corvette?"

"Uncle Sam's. Used to belong to a pill smuggler in Juarez."

Ryan nodded. "And you're out of Houston?"

Ochoa nodded. "Got in late last night."

"Come on back." Ryan led the way down the hall. "Did they tell you what I'm working on?"

"Banner, the strip-searcher of Senator Cowden's granddaughter."

Ryan opened the door for the IA agent, and then followed him into the office. "He's tried the same thing with four others. How did we end up with the likes of him? ATF is still laughing. We got him from them, you know." Ryan made it sound accusatory.

"It was a mistake." The IA agent agreed, and sipped his coffee.

Ryan stared, waiting for more from the branch of Customs charged with ferreting out the Chuck Banners before they were hired, but Ochoa only stared back. Ryan decided to drop it for now. He opened his briefcase and took out a tan file folder and tossed it onto the desk. "This is the statement of the senator's granddaughter, Jill Cowden, 16 years old, lives in San Antonio. Banner made her strip completely naked then grabbed her breasts. Her statement isn't signed yet. I'll take care of it on the way back to D.C."

Ryan removed another folder and dropped it on top of the other one. "Marsha Horton from San Diego. Banner forced her to expose herself. Her statement was taken by phone. It's been faxed to the San Diego office for her signature, should be back by special delivery in a few days."

He added another folder to the pile. "A local fourteen-year-old, Lupe Martinez. She wouldn't take her clothes off, so Banner felt her up and let her go. It's signed. So is this one." He looked at the folder containing Sarah's statement. "A woman from Socorro, New Mexico, still in town temporarily. She refused to go into the search room. The only one that got away." Ryan tossed the folder onto the desk. "There's one other known victim, a Mexican woman working as a cook and housekeeper for Mexican Immigration inspectors at the dam. I'm having trouble getting permission from the Mexicans to interview her. We'll give it another day then ask headquarters to make a call to Mexico City."

Ochoa was non-committal, nodding as he arranged the folders in fan formation. Ryan didn't care for this lethargic attitude. "I think it's time to talk to Banner," he continued. "He checked me as I came across the river yesterday, said he wanted his attorney and union rep when he was interviewed. That's when I asked for you." Ryan was beginning to wonder why.

Ochoa broke his silence. "If you're going after him administratively he's required to answer all questions and is entitled to union representation but no attorney. If you're going to charge him with a criminal violation, he gets the Miranda warning, an attorney, and... he doesn't have to say a damned thing." Ochoa glared at him.

Ryan stared back. There was hostility here, not disinterest or laziness. Ochoa was pissed about something. Ryan relaxed. He could handle anger, but not dead weight. He would straighten it out later. Ryan closed his silver briefcase and hoisted it from the desk. "Look the statements over. Banner is coming off the rolls. Administrative case, criminal case, whatever it takes – he's gone. Personally, I'd like to see him do jail time. I'm staying at the Ramada. Give me a call tonight."

♦   ♦   ♦

Paulson's boat-repair shop was on the east side of the highway, a mile past the Ramada. Ryan noticed the shop's large double-doors were closed as he pulled up beside the Ranchero with the Whaler on its trailer. Sarah stepped out of the Ford and into the Dodge. The pleasant smell from yesterday was back.

"Closed," she said and shrugged. Last night at dinner she had talked about having Paulson check the outboard motor for possible damage from the water and Coleman lantern fuel. "I think it will be all right." She looked at Ryan and wrinkled her forehead. "It ran fine when I brought it in yesterday. Where do you want to leave your car?"

Before he could answer, a black Mercedes pulled up behind them, the rattle of its diesel engine reverberating from the closed metal garage doors. A short, middle-aged man in a western straw hat and tan guayabera shirt got out and stared at the closed shop.

"That's Señor Fuentes," Sarah said, "the federal policeman." She opened the car door and shouted his name.

The man turned from the building and Ryan saw his face light up. "Miss Sarah," he said, coming toward them.

Ryan opened his door and got out. Contacts had always been the name of the game in his work, and he seldom ignored such an opportunity. He passed between the Dodge and the rattling Mercedes, noticing the alert young driver and that no armament was visible inside the vehicle. Armed Mexican feds were waved through the port of entry when Ryan was on the border. At least one AK-47 would have been on the seat beside the driver or on the floorboard.

"No, nothing at all," Sarah was saying as Ryan approached. "What about the mayor?"

"*Nada*," the *federale* said, shaking his head. He was a good three inches shorter than Sarah. "We are still looking, but early this morning one of the Coast Guard boats from Matamoros got stuck on an island."

Oh my...." Sarah made sympathetic head-shaking motions before introducing Ryan to Armando Fuentes.

"*Con mucho gusto*." Ryan said as they shook hands.

"*¿Agente de Aduana?*" Fuentes asked, as if he wasn't sure of what Sarah had said.

"Yes, customs agent," Ryan said in Spanish. Fuentes was polite but didn't appear to be impressed.

"Well, I have to find this man." He gestured toward the boat shop. "They... the Park Rangers," he gestured northward, the direction of park headquarters, "they told me this is the man who operates the machinery that can lift the boat off the island."

"That's right," Sarah nodded. "He has a crane barge. But as you can see, he's not here this morning."

The *federale* shook his head, glancing impatiently around.

"I know where we might find him," Ryan said. "It will only take a minute to find out." Ryan opened the rear passenger door of the Dodge. Fuentes stared up at him for a moment, then signaled the Mercedes driver to follow and got in. Ryan winked at Sarah. She got into the front seat and closed the door.

◆　◆　◆

Customs Agent Tom Del Castillo and Greg Paulson emerged from Betty's Ranch House Cafe as Ryan rolled into the parking lot. "He is the thin man with white hair," Ryan said in Spanish as he stopped beside

Tom's car. He and Fuentes got out of the Dodge. "Customer for you," Ryan said as Paulson and Tom approached. Both red-eyed and unshaven, they had obviously been up all night. Tom had worked his gun smuggling case. As Ryan stared into Paulson's tired face, he had no doubt he was looking at the deliveryman on the machine gun case. "This is Armando Fuentes, Mexican Federal Judicial Police. He has a boat stuck on an island." Ryan turned to Fuentes and gestured toward the other two men. "Señor Fuentes, Greg Paulson and Customs Agent Tom Del Castillo."

They shook hands and Paulson asked where the boat was aground.

"A little west of the dam."

Paulson nodded. "Lifted a boat off there Monday morning. Been lifting them off all summer. Mexico ought to put a lighted buoy there." He stared at Fuentes for a moment, then at Ryan. "Flat-top island, only two feet out of the water when the lake is up, invisible after dark. If you follow the channel markers, you're OK, but that makes for a zigzag course, so everybody takes the short cut from marker two to marker six." He shook his head. "Still OK unless you drift south a little, then you're high and dry." He turned toward a nearby pickup and motioned. "Let's go get it."

The black Mercedes was waiting nearby. Fuentes motioned for it and turned to Ryan. "*Grácias*," he said shaking Ryan's hand. "If I can return the favor...."

"I have been trying to arrange an appointment with the chief of Mexican Immigration," Ryan said quickly in Spanish. "I know he is a very busy man, but I need only a moment of his time."

The f*ederale* stopped the handshake, but did not release Ryan's hand. "Would you like to see him today? I can make the call."

"Tomorrow will be fine." Fuentes could do more than get him an appointment. Ryan went for it. "I only need permission to speak to a woman who works at the dam."

"What is her name?" Fuentes dropped Ryan's hand and motioned his driver out of the car.

Ryan gave him the woman's name. "She's a housekeeper and cook for the Immigration inspectors."

Fuentes nodded to his driver and waited as the young man wrote in a small notebook. "You will see her tomorrow," he said and leaned into the open driver's door of the Dodge. "So nice to see you again, Miss Sarah." He touched his hat, got into the rear seat of the Mercedes and was gone in a cloud of diesel smoke.

"How did it go last night?" Ryan turned to Tom, now staring down through the windshield at Sarah.

"Good, got everyone on their way about three this morning. They're holed up in a San Antonio motel surrounded by ATF." He managed a smile. "They'll probably move on to Houston tonight." Tom took a deep breath and looked back at Sarah. Ryan led him to the passenger side of the car and introduced him to Sarah with a brief explanation. "I thought I had seen you before," Tom said as they shook hands through the window, "At Paulson's, I believe."

"He keeps my old boat running." Sarah said.

"Ours, too," Tom said. "The two Customs boats and my own."

There was a moment of silence, then Tom said he had better get some sleep. "Nice meeting you," he said to Sarah. Ryan followed him toward his car.

"Tom, I need to borrow a rifle."

"Sure," Tom said with no hesitation. He pulled car keys from his pocket and turned toward the trunk of the car. "How about a machine gun? I've got a 9mm Aug right here."

"No, I don't know anything about Augs. I need a rifle. How about your M-1?"

"No problem. You want it right now?" He turned back to the driver's door and unlocked it.

"Yes, if you don't mind. We'll pick up Sarah's boat and Ranchero and be right out. We also have a couple of questions about the lake."

"Come on," Tom said, getting into his car. He was a good man, Ryan thought, not one question about the rifle or Sarah.

17

Ryan watched from the dock as the trailer submerged and the Boston Whaler floated free of its padded trailer cradle. Ryan pulled the boat toward him with the long bow line. Sarah drove the Ranchero and trailer to the top of the ramp, parked and hurried back down the incline, forcing herself to take long steps. She was wearing tight jeans again, a tan, long-sleeve shirt, and a billed turquoise cap she had bought last night as Ryan purchased his own lake attire: blue jeans, blue T-shirt, white sneakers, and a black baseball cap with mesh sides. Sarah stepped into the boat without breaking stride. Ryan followed, pushing away from the dock with one foot. Their search for the Lost Caracol gold mine was underway.

"This is where the old highway crossed," Sarah said. "This boat ramp was part of State 290. The Volkswagen was parked over there." She pointed across the canyon to a mott of trees just above the waterline. The abandoned highway, marked by old guard posts, descended southward along the face of the limestone cliff and ended at the trees. That is where the machine guns were to be delivered before the change in plans. It was also, as they learned from Tom that morning, where the old treasure hunter had been camped. Ryan glanced upriver. Half a mile away, the high bridge now spanning the Pecos glistened in the morning sun.

The Whaler's motor gurgled to life and pushed the boat slowly past the end of the dock. Ryan sat on the padded starboard bench. Sarah was all business standing behind the wheel, glancing to either side and the rear as she reversed the motor allowing an approaching boat to turn into the dock.

"Good morning," she yelled to the two border patrolmen in the boat. "How's it going?"

"Good," one of them answered as he cut the motor. "They found the red kayak in Castle Canyon. The search has been moved over there."

Sarah waved, nodded and gave Ryan a knowing look. "Would you believe that's on the Devil's River side of the lake?" She pushed the throttle forward and turned downriver.

It made no sense for the boy's kayak to be thirty or forty miles away from his car, unless someone took it there. If Tom hadn't had the Volkswagen towed, would it also have been found on the other side of the lake? Or south of Ciudad Acuña like the treasure hunter's pickup?

Ryan glanced at the steering console. His .45 and the walkie-talkie were inside. Tom's M-1 and a hundred rounds of ammunition were in the bow storage area. He was glad now that he had brought along the firepower for this one-day expedition even though he thought there was little danger with search teams saturating this area of the lake. Now, the searchers had pulled out. He felt concern until he remembered the Mexicans. Fuentes and his men would still be here in the Rio Grande. Two more boats passed, headed north toward the dock they had just left.

Morning freshness was still in the canyon. Ryan rubbed goose bumps from his bare arms as they sped southward. The canyon wall on the right was suddenly gone. "Rio Grande," Sarah shouted above the wind and motor noise.

The Rio Grande, now combined with the Pecos, was wider and straight as far west as Ryan could see. "The old railroad bridge crossed there." Sarah looked back and made a sweeping motion with her arm across what were the last few yards of the Pecos River. The west wall seemed to emerge from the water, and they were in the Rio Grande River Canyon. The old abandoned railroad-right-of-way was visible as a wide ledge along the cliffs on the U.S. side.

Sarah was taking them to the railroad tunnel. Directions from there were sketchy. Patterson and his fiancée had searched together for three days before she left. The girl said she was convinced that the mine was now underwater.

"Parida Cave," Sarah pointed left, "where the railroaders camped. It's an archaeological site now."

Ryan nodded and turned toward the huge hollow in the cliff. A small boat dock had been built just below the cave. No trace of the old railroad here, but it must have passed nearby. They moved on without slowing. Two miles downriver, Sarah veered left and cut the motor to idle. "Here's the tunnel." The boat coasted toward a steep outcrop. Ryan looked for an opening but saw none until he followed Sarah's gaze down to water level. Only three feet of the flooded tunnel entrance was visible.

"It's about a hundred feet long," Sarah said. "The old right of way is visible again downriver, climbs out of the canyon and turns east."

Ryan looked across the wide Rio Grande for a place where the hunter and laborers might have climbed out of the canyon after rafting across. According to the file, the party traveled inland after crossing the river until they again encountered the river. Sarah's maps showed how that was possible. Downriver from the tunnel, the Rio Grande made sweeping bends to the north, east and south, forming a half-circle two miles in diameter. On a ledge in a side canyon, near the point where they struck the river again, the two laborers were lowered into a deep, narrow hole to retrieve the bear. In the process, they discovered gold.

"Let's cruise the other side," Ryan suggested.

Sarah backed the boat away from the tunnel, crossed to the other side and turned downriver. The canyon wall on the Mexican side glowed reddish-brown, sometimes almost pink – beautiful in the morning sun. It opened to numerous inlets that could afford access to the mesa above.

"Seminole Canyon," Sarah said. "Two miles in there is where I ran out of lantern fuel the other night."

Ryan looked across the river. The wide mouth of the intersecting canyon formed a large, funnel-shaped cove in an otherwise-solid wall. On the southern lip, a small boat dock jutted from a brushy knoll in front of a deep overhang.

"Panther Cave," Sarah said. "Another pictograph site."

The canyon and the cave were marked on Sarah's maps, almost halfway around the half-circle formed by the river. They had decided last night that this was the place to begin the search. Tom had indicated this as the general area where Jimmy had collected his petrified snails. Everything seemed to match up.

Ryan turned to the Mexican side, ready to find the intersecting canyon. It would be a cove now, like the mouth of Seminole Canyon. The boat surged forward.

"Let's go on to Chango's," Sarah said. "He'll know where to find petrified snails if anyone does. He could save us a lot of time."

Ryan nodded, leaned back, and watched the pink wall flow past. He had felt a twinge of envy last night as Sarah went on and on about this half-Anglo Mexican who had been so helpful to her. He was anxious to meet this wonderful person.

The pink wall opened occasionally, sometimes widely. It would take days to take even a cursory look at all these possibilities. Sarah pointed out the large cove where her sister's cap had been found and where the mayor's boat was last seen. Naked people. Were they naked when they disappeared? This is the first place they would look.

The wall opened up several more times, and then Sarah turned into the largest cove yet. It was almost a mile wide and remained so for several minutes, then cliffs loomed ahead and Ryan saw a large, blue and white houseboat moored in front of a large natural shelter formed by an overhanging bluff. A row of weathered power poles descending from a nearby hill ended near the houseboat. Electricity and even a telephone line here?

"I don't see his boat," Sarah said looking around as she cut the motor to idle. The Whaler knifed through the water toward the dock in front of the houseboat. "I really wanted to talk to him before we started looking." She had hardly spoken before a dark man wearing a red-and-blue striped T-shirt appeared on the deck of the houseboat. Ryan extended his right foot, cushioned the boat's contact with the dock and stepped onto the wooden planks.

"Where's your boat?" Sarah shouted.

"*Federales* took it," the man shouted back as he stepped onto the narrow dock.

"The same ones who took my pistol?" Sarah was on the dock now, hands on hips, looking and sounding feisty.

"I'm sorry about that." The man walked quickly toward them. "There was nothing I could do. I tried to pass you up, but they insisted on checking you out. They caught me at the marina that morning, made me run the boat for them all day."

"And then kept it?"

Chango nodded. "The Coast Guard from Matamoros came in yesterday. The *federales* wanted something that would keep up with them."

Ryan leaned over to tie up the Whaler.

"This is Ryan Shaw, a friend of mine from Socorro." Sarah said. "Ryan, this is Robert Andrews, a very good friend who has been a big help to me."

Ryan straightened, somewhat surprised to learn he was from New Mexico, and shook hands with Robert Andrews. Ryan judged the man to be about thirty-five. Pale blue eyes, olive complexion and dark curly hair gave him the appearance of an Eastern European. Trim and muscular, he stood several inches shorter than Ryan. The dense black hair covering his arms accounted for his nickname.

"Most people call me Chango," he said.

Literally "monkey" in Spanish, Chango was a common nickname along the border for people with heavy body hair. "Nice to meet you, Chango." Ryan smiled. He wouldn't mind calling Robert Andrews a monkey at all.

"Come on up to the store and have some coffee." Chango shaded his eyes and glanced at the sun. "Or a beer. Lunch will be ready soon." He led them off the dock and up a steep path to the hollow in the cliff. Sarah's spiel about railroad crews using a natural shelter for a construction camp did nothing to prepare him for what this gymnasium-sized overhang contained: shelves of canned goods, metal storage bins, kitchen cabinets, a sink, a cooking range and a refrigerator lined the back wall of what appeared to be the occupied area of the huge cave. Metal card tables, folding chairs and cots were scattered randomly about. Most impressive was the room-size walk-in freezer extending from the back wall, partitioning off the living area.

"That's where we freeze the catch," Chango volunteered, apparently noticing Ryan's interest in the freezer. "The fish are kept in live traps at the camps and brought here once a week, dressed out and frozen. We haul out a couple of tons a month." Chango motioned toward the shelves of canned goods and storage bins. "I keep a few things here for the fishermen and their families. It's a long way into town." He surveyed the shelter as if seeing it for the first time. "This was where we used to keep hay. I used to have a ranch here – did Sarah tell you?"

Ryan said yes, noticing the telephone pager clipped to Chango's belt. In Mexico, rural telephones were expensive, therefore something of an oddity. Ryan had been surprised to see power and telephone lines here – now a pager?

"The government took my ranch when the dam was built," Chango said. "The house my great-grandfather built is down there." He stared toward the cove. "Under twenty feet of water. All they gave me was fishing rights for 6,000 acres along the river, and I still have to give them half of the catch... like this was a goddamned catfish mine."

That seemed a strange remark from someone not in the mining business or even a mining area. "The power lines were originally for the ranch then?" Ryan asked.

"Yes." Chango turned his attention back to the shelter. "They wouldn't let me build on park land, so I had to make do."

Nearby, two stout young women were busy around the gas range and cabinets. Smoke and steam rose and dissipated long before reaching the high limestone ceiling. Whatever was cooking was going to be delicious. Chango motioned them toward a long wooden dining table and led the way. "Coffee for everyone," he shouted in Spanish and then looked back. "Unless you want a beer."

Coffee would be fine, Ryan and Sarah agreed as they sat down at the table. On a blanket nearby, two chubby, naked toddlers played with tin cups and plates. They had dark curly hair and blue eyes, like Chango. Ryan looked for other similarities, then concluded it was none of his business who they belonged to and turned to the mug of coffee that had been placed before him. It was typically very sweet and strong.

Chango asked about Sarah's search. She gave what sounded like her standard negative reply, sharing nothing about the file on the treasure with him. Ryan thought that was interesting, since Chango was supposed to be so helpful.

"We're looking for petrified snails today," Sarah said. "Thought you might know where we could find some."

For just an instant, Chango stopped stirring his coffee. "Can't help you there," he said without looking up. "Seashell and tree fossils are everywhere." He tightened his lips and shook his head, "No snails, never seen any of those."

There was a long silence. Ryan thought it odd that there was no question of why someone searching for loved ones would suddenly be interested in fossil snails.

The sound of hoof beats ended the strange awkwardness. Ryan turned in his chair toward the open side of the shelter and watched a small, slender man dismount from a glistening dapple-gray mare. The man's dusty boots found the ground lightly. He dropped the bridle reins to the ground and stepped into the shade. Chango excused himself and went to meet the horseman.

"That man is ninety-two years old," Sarah whispered. "Did you see how he swung off that horse? Just watch the way he rides when he leaves. The man is amazing."

"Ninety-two," Ryan repeated, as he looked closer at the conversing pair. Chango was a full head taller. The crown of the rider's narrow brimmed straw hat was just even with the top of Chango's head as they turned and walked toward the tables.

As he arrived, the horseman removed his hat. "Miss Sarah", he greeted her with a nod and a smile. "Señor," he turned toward Ryan.

"Ryan, this is Monte. Monte, Ryan Shaw, a friend of Sarah's from Socorro."

"Ryan," Monte repeated as they shook hands. "Ryan," he said again, staring.

Ryan noted that Monte had quite a grip for a man of any age.

"Monte takes care of our now-mini-ranch. An old man like this can handle what's left of it now." Chango laughed sarcastically and slapped Monte's back. "Sit and finish your coffee. We'll be right back". Chango and Monte walked toward the back of the overhang area.

"So, does this old Monte have a last name?" Ryan asked when they had gone.

"Del Monte is all he goes by, all I have ever heard except for the shortened version, Monte. He was a close pal of Chango's grandfather. The grandfather told Chango that the man came out of the brush one day and no one could pronounce his name so they just called him Señor Del Monte. That's the story, all I know."

"Well, old Del Monte has a telephone pager on his belt, just like Chango." Ryan commented.

"What do you mean?"

"Oh, nothing, I guess. In a country with few telephones. I suppose a pager would be handy for a lot of things."

Sarah was still looking puzzled when Chango and Monte returned.

"Have a good day, Mr. Shaw, Miss Sarah." Monte said as he passed. Ryan returned the greeting and watched as Monte gathered the bridle reins and sprang gracefully into a high stirrup. He swung into the saddle and moved the mare away at a walk for a few yards then into an easy canter. Any signal to the animal from Monte was imperceptible. The old man was part of his horse.

"Well," Sarah broke the silence, "we are going to look for petrified snails. A kid in town has some, claims he found them south of the railroad tunnel. They do look unusual. If they were polished up, they might sell in my store."

"Never seen any." Chango looked toward the cove, closing the subject.

The two women served beans, rice, fried catfish, flour tortillas and freshly made salsa. The salsa was hot and delicious, as was all the fare. Sarah and Chango chatted about the weather, the missing sailboat and a shepherd boy neither of them had seen for a while. Ryan ate and watched the toddlers. Chango never asked what business Ryan was in or what he was doing in the area.

♦   ♦   ♦

"I think they're his," Sarah said after turning the boat away from Chango's dock.

"What?"

"The babies. You were staring at them the whole time we were there. I think they belong to Chango. The two women are sisters, not married or living with any of the fishermen." She shrugged. "That's all I know about it." Sarah smiled, removed the baseball cap and let the wind blow through her short hair. Auburn, Ryan thought. Perhaps a little too dark for auburn. Whatever the color, it was just right.

He thought about the way she had handled herself with Chango. "What was all that about back there?

"What?"

"Why am I suddenly from Socorro, for one thing?"

"It made things a little more relaxed. He doesn't have much use for government officials from either side of the border. I thought of it at the last minute. I knew you could handle it.

"Thanks. Why didn't you tell him the real reason we were looking for snails?"

Sarah gave him a surprised look. "Because he lied. Didn't you notice the way he acted when I asked about them?"

"I noticed." Ryan smiled. Chango was no longer Mr. Wonderful. "I also noticed you didn't tell him you were leaving Saturday. Not going to tell him goodbye?"

She scrutinized the water ahead, turned north into the main channel and shoved the throttle forward. "No, I don't want to tell Chango goodbye," she shouted over the wind and motor sounds. "Or anyone else around here."

Ryan was not sure he understood her last comment until he saw the sad look on Sarah's face as she glanced briefly back at him. He could hardly hear her and moved closer.

"The damned IRS," she said softly now that he was near. "They will take my store, the lawyers said, if I don't show up this time. It's such a mess, a big mistake, a three-year battle. I don't want to go... for a lot of reasons, but I'm not giving up my store... or anything else." She turned her head slightly, and Ryan could see a smile.

He absorbed that bit of information along with the smile and found it quite pleasing. When he was done with the Banner case he just might head west for a few days. He shifted his position, improving his view of her.

♦   ♦   ♦

The goat herd grazed on a narrow green meadow between the low bluffs and the lake. Sarah veered toward them, leaned over to Ryan and said, "Now we'll find out where the petrified snails are." Only then did Ryan see the boy in a crumpled straw hat, waving and running toward them.

18

Sarah cut the motor and nosed the boat into the grass-covered silt. More than two weeks had passed since she had seen Mario and his herd of goats. "*¿Que tal?*" she shouted. "How have you been?" She moved to the bow of the boat and jumped down.

"Good, there was rain to the west. I took the goats there for a few days." Mario spoke only Spanish. Between him and Chango, Sarah's Spanish had improved dramatically during the last two months. She now conversed fluently on most ordinary subjects.

Ryan came up behind them. "This is Ryan Shaw," Sarah said in Spanish. "Ryan, this is Mario, a very special friend. His father found the red cap that came from my store." She chose her words carefully, a little intimidated. Ryan's native exchanges with Armando Fuentes earlier had impressed her.

"With much pleasure," Ryan said in Spanish as he shook Mario's hand. "That's a fine herd of goats. How many do you have?"

"Sixty-six." Mario's answer was quick. "Thirty nannies, thirty-four kids, and two billies."

Ryan gazed at the animals as if he were going to make a purchase. "Fine goats," he repeated, and turned to Sarah.

Yes – she should be the one to ask about the snails.

"You are helping look for Miss Sarah's sister and brother-in-law?" Mario asked.

"Yes, and today we are also looking for something else."

"I know what happened to the people on the sailboat," Mario said, turning to Sarah. "They were shot."

Sarah understood, but hesitated, running it through her mind again. By the time she was sure, Ryan had asked Mario how he knew, and Mario was explaining.

"I saw it! Just before sundown, in the cove, where the cap was found." He pointed upriver. "Someone shooting the people on the big sailboat. Two women were shot when I got there. Then I saw a man on a hill above the cliffs get shot. Then a man came out of the cabin on the sailboat. He was looking at the women when he was shot. That was when I ran away. The next day, airplanes and boats came. They were everywhere. I stayed away."

Sarah was stunned. People on the sailboat shot, and a man – the student. She seemed to be growing numb. Vaguely, she heard Ryan telling Mario that he had done right in running and staying away from the lake. "We want to hear the whole story," Ryan's voice was sounding louder. "Let's move out of the sun. Would you like a Pepsi or a Coca-Cola?"

The question brought Sarah back, turned her toward the boat. "I'll get it," she said. Mario liked Pepsi, and she had oranges, apples and candy bars for him. He said it had happened just before sundown. God, she had almost been in the middle of it.

They found shade below the bluffs. Sarah listened to Ryan take Mario back to Sunday afternoon again, and with his investigator's interviewing skills extract every detail the boy could possibly remember. She was remembering events that day and the night before as well: the turning doorknob, a dead motor, waves slapping the hull of the drifting boat, a waiting rifleman. She looked across the breadth of water, wondering if a rifle bullet could reach them from the opposite canyon rim. She noticed Ryan was giving their surroundings the same careful scrutiny. The back of her neck began to tingle, and she shivered. Instead of moving out into the warm sun, she edged deeper into the shadow of the cliff.

Mario again repeated that the shots had come from the south side of the cove, and that he had seen no one. Whoever did the shooting was behind the rocks or under the thick brush. Finally, Ryan seemed satisfied, turned to Sarah and asked if she had any questions. "No." She could think of no questions Mario could answer. Her mind was on the long days she had spent alone, in the boat and on foot, prowling that mile-long, wedge-shaped inlet. Laura and Mike had died there. She could easily have died there, too. A hundred times over she might have been gunned down like the others. She shuddered.

Ryan gave her a questioning look, then asked Mario about the snails. Snails... she had forgotten about the snails.

"*El mismo lugar*, the same place," Mario said. "On the north side. When the water is low there are many fossil snails, some loose, like gravel, some in the rock."

Ryan looked at Sarah, winked and smiled, turned back to Mario and asked him about his family. Mario's father, mother and three older brothers made up one of Chango's fishing camps. Mario, the youngest, tended the family's herd of goats, illegally grazing it on Mexican federal parkland. Sarah already knew all of this. She continued staring quietly at the cliffs across the river, her mind hazy as Ryan quickly drew out from Mario what had taken her weeks to piece together.

"Stay out of sight," Ryan warned, "and don't tell anyone but your family what you have told us." He patted the boy's shoulder. "Understand?"

Mario said he understood. Ryan looked at Sarah. "Let's go before someone sees him with us."

Sarah didn't fully understand, but she was ready to go. She said goodbye to Mario and walked to the boat.

♦   ♦   ♦

Sarah was not aware that Ryan was standing behind her until he reached around and pulled the throttle back. The boat settled into a glide.

"Where are we going in such a hurry?" he asked.

"The cove is just ahead, but...." She didn't want to go there, hadn't realized the boat was going almost full speed. The image of Laura and Mike being ambushed would not leave her, would never leave her.

"The cove is where people are being murdered," Ryan said.

"Yes, I know now. That's what happened to Laura and Mike. It could have happened to me, anytime. I was there every day for more than a week after the cap was found, and I've been back almost every evening, cruising the shoreline. I must have left there only minutes before those people were killed Sunday."

"Don't ever go there alone again." Ryan leaned over, opened the door in the steering console and pulled out the walkie-talkie. He turned it on, called for the Del Rio office several times, then any Del Rio unit, but got no answer. He frowned, glanced at the high cliffs on the U.S. side, and put the radio back inside the console. "Sit down. I'll drive for awhile."

She sat on the port-side bench, saw Ryan look up toward the canyon rim again.

"If I can get up there with the radio," he said. "I can get some help out here to watch our backs while we look around the cove." As he spoke, he adjusted the throttle and the boat moved slowly upriver.

Who was going to watch their backs? She leaned over to ask. The throb of a powerful engine erupted from behind them. She looked back. A huge vessel had rounded a bend not far behind. It appeared to be some sort of military boat. Ryan maneuvered the Whaler to the right as the gray, barge-like craft quickly overtook them. As it pushed past, a dozen men in helmets and olive-drab fatigues stared over the gunwale. The Mexican flag fluttered from the stern. Chango's sleek, red-and-white outboard followed closely behind. Federal Judicial Policeman Armando Fuentes waved from his stern seat in Chango's boat. A driver and two other men stared straight ahead.

Sarah and Ryan returned the greeting. Ryan moved the Whaler into the huge, churning wake and followed. Sarah saw Chango's boat pass the barge and lead it into the cove she knew so well.

Ryan pulled the throttle back to idle and turned to her. "Let's give them a few minutes." He said.

A few minutes for what? She hadn't understood anything since talking to Mario.

"That must be the Coast Guard boat that ran aground," Ryan said. "Maybe they'll come up with something."

"And if they don't?"

Ryan shrugged. "I'll try to get a couple of agents out here to sit on the cliffs while we look around."

"Right, U.S. Customs is going into Mexico with us to search for a lost gold mine."

Ryan's face dropped, and he looked away.

She could see her words had offended. She hadn't intended them to sound so sarcastic. "Sorry, guess I've been at this alone too long. I'm not accustomed to anything but excuses from anyone."

It was as if her remark and apology had never happened. Ryan put his hand on the steering wheel. "Let's see what's going on. Even a psycho wouldn't attack a Coast Guard ship." He reached for the throttle. "Remember, not a word about anything Mario told us. The boy has no useful information, can't identify anyone, but this is a political hot potato. If Fuentes finds out Mario witnessed the shooting, the boy could be forced to say anything. It wouldn't be pleasant for Mario or his family."

Sarah was familiar with horror stories about Mexican interrogations. Ryan was right, Mario should be protected. How fortunate someone was thinking of that. The Whaler moved slowly toward the cove. Sarah leaned back and gave Customs Special Agent Ryan Shaw a long, appraising look.

Ray Summers

19

The red and white sixteen-footer was tied below the cliffs on the south side of the cove. Armando Fuentes shouted something Sarah could not understand and motioned them to approach Chango's boat. As they approached with excess speed, Ryan put the Whaler into reverse too soon, kept it there too long and accidentally killed the motor. All of which left them drifting in the wrong direction several yards from Fuentes and his men.

"Give it to the woman," Fuentes shouted in Spanish and laughed. "She is the good driver."

Sarah watched Ryan smile, shake his head and catch the line thrown by the young man in the bow of the other boat. As they were pulled alongside, Sarah recognized the two men in brown uniforms. They had been with Chango on Monday morning. The thin-faced man who had taken her pistol raised his chin and gave her a sour look. She did the same to him.

"Welcome," Fuentes said in English. "We are having a late lunch. Please join us." He held up a bulging tortilla and mumbled something in Spanish to the young man.

"No, thank you," Sarah said. "We have already eaten." Even as she spoke, Ryan was saying the same thing in Spanish and accepting two brown bottles of beer from the young man. He twisted the cap from one bottle, winked and handed it to her. What was all this winking?

Fuentes introduced the young man, Miguel Flores, as his driver. The other two were Mexican Customs inspector: George Gomez, the stocky one with leering eyes, and Rafael Orosco, the thin-faced man who had taken her pistol. Even now, his dark, rodent-like eyes were on the brown briefcase strapped to the Whaler's steering console.

"*¡Salud!*" Ryan held up his beer. Sarah and the others did the same. Sarah held her breath. She was not a beer drinker and could hardly stand the smell of it. When everyone else turned up their bottles, she sipped. Definitely not Chablis, but what the hell, it was ice cold. She took a big swallow and managed not to shudder.

"The Coast Guard from Matamoros," Fuentes said in Spanish, pointing his beer bottle at the barge moving sluggishly toward the main channel. "They have electronic instruments to see the bottom, and divers to investigate, but there is nothing here. This water is only five meters deep. We measured it yesterday. If the boat were here, the masts would be above the water." He laughed. "Or something would be floating around."

"This is where the cap that belonged to Miss Dobbs' sister was found," Ryan said.

"Oh – this is the place?" Fuentes looked at her. She nodded. Fuentes knew about the cap. She had gone to him when it was found. Like the FBI, Mexican Federal Judicial Police have enforcement jurisdiction over federal parks and reservations. Also like his U.S. counterparts, Fuentes had cited lack of funding and manpower as reasons for not initiating a search. He did assign a federal game warden to look over the cove and gave Sarah permission to continue on her own for as long as she wished.

Fuentes surveyed the cove, as if considering what he had just learned about the cap, as if he might make the connection, and then he leaned over and took a bite from the bulging taco, dripping grease and salsa onto Chango's maroon deck carpeting. Sarah was considering telling him about the mine when Ryan spoke. "You have found nothing?"

"*Nada*," Fuentes replied, and drank from his beer bottle. "We had the soldiers here yesterday. They looked everywhere." He made a sweeping motion with the remains of the taco, then popped it into his mouth. He shook his head, chewing. "There is nothing here. I told the captain..." – he gestured toward the huge boat, now almost out of sight – "but this is where he wants to start." He shook his head again, turned and selected another taco from the grease-stained paper bag on the seat beside him.

"Mind if we look?" Ryan asked.

This man wastes no time, Sarah thought, but what better time than when the Coast Guard is here? Unconsciously, she sipped from the beer bottle and grimaced.

"You are my guests, look all you want." Fuentes made another sweeping motion, this time with his beer bottle. Thin Face was not eating or drinking. Sarah noticed him fold his arms and glare across the cove, not pleased with Fuentes' invitation to outsiders.

"I have units searching between here and the dam," Fuentes said. "That is where the sailboat will be found." He nodded. "We will join them shortly." He finished his beer and tossed the bottle overboard. The young man held out another almost before the empty hit the water.

"The Coast Guard going with you?" Ryan asked.

"After the captain has checked everything, even where the bottom is visible." Fuentes gave a contemptuous chuckle. "Then he will come to the big canyons west of the dam. That is where the sailboat is, in the deep water."

Ryan thanked Fuentes and the others, accepted two more brown bottles, and turned to Sarah. "How about taking us across the cove?"

Sarah smiled. He had surrendered command gracefully. She stood up and handed him her beer. "I'm through with this." She stepped to the wheel, hit the starter, let the motor idle long enough to give Rat Face her best conceited smirk. She backed the Whaler away. She knew just the place to start.

20

The bow of the Whaler crunched onto the gravel bar in front of the bluff. Sarah had beached the boat here before. She pointed to a mesquite stub protruding from the wall. Ryan finished the beer she had donated and jumped down with the bowline.

"You're not going to get drunk again, are you?" Sarah asked with a smile.

"Not on two beers," he replied. "The other two are in the cooler – and I wasn't drunk the other night. Someone spilled beer on me, a whole can." He turned to tie up the boat.

"And who might that have been? Some woman in a bar?" Sarah froze, not believing what she had just said. Whoever spilled beer on this man was none of her business. She opened her mouth to say so, but he was on the beach beside the bow, looking up at her. "Well, it was a woman," he said, seriously, "but it wasn't in any bar." He winked and turned away.

Winking, what's that about? She tried to remember when it had started.

"No snails here," he said, scrutinizing the ten-foot bluff in front of them. "And this is just plain gravel." He kicked the ground. "Mario said the water had to be low. Maybe this is just a shelf."

"It is deep here," she said. Wondering about spilled beer had pushed the winking mystery from her mind. She unfastened the briefcase from the steering console, placed it on the port-side bench seat and opened it. Maybe Rat Face was watching with binoculars. She hoped so. She left the small pistol in its black vinyl case and tried to push it under her waistband. It had always fit before, but these new jeans were tight. She hadn't worn anything so tight since college. What was she doing in them now? So what if she had accidentally taken off a few pounds and could slip into a size four. Why the sudden shopping for clothes?

"Take it out of the case and stick it in your hip pocket," Ryan said as he turned to look along the cliff. "I think we can get up through that washed-out place."

"We can. I've been up there – and higher, all along the cliffs on both sides of the cove and I don't remember a hole large enough for a bear to fall into." She shoved the pistol into her right hip pocket. It was a snug fit.

"Then let's look for something else."

"What?" She moved to the bow of the boat and jumped down.

"I really wanted to start on the other side, where Mario said the shots came from, but with you and Slim making faces at each other, I thought we had best get away."

She thought he was going to wink again, but he only smiled. "He's the creep who took my pistol."

"And Fuentes got it back for you?" The blue-green eyes seemed to darken and bore through her. She tried not to look away, but that look was unnerving. She had to get away from those eyes. She glanced down, brushing something imaginary from her jeans. "Yes, I mentioned that my pistol had been confiscated when I told him about the sailboat."

"That was good," he said seriously. "Very good. I was raised on the border and you're the only person I've ever heard of to get something back from Mexican Customs."

She looked up at him. The eyes were friendly again. He tightened his mouth and nodded. "And a pistol at that." He shook his head and chuckled.

Sarah felt her face flush. How silly, she thought.

The Coast Guard barge made another pass headed for the end of the cove. Across the way, Chango's boat cranked up and sped away in the opposite direction. The *federales* had finished lunch.

Sarah followed Ryan up the washed-out notch onto the bluff, which in reality was a wide shelf along the brown cliffs towering some thirty feet above them. "This goes all the way to the end of the cove." She pointed to lighter-colored cliffs two hundred yards away. "That's where the sailboat was anchored."

Ryan nodded. "Can we get around to the other side?"

"Yes, but we'll have to go up first, all the way to the top. There's a passageway near the head of the canyon." She went around him and led the way along the shelf. On previous trips, she had been watchful only for snakes and scorpions. Now she glanced frequently across the cove at the brush-covered mesa above the cliffs. Mario said the shots had come from there. The throb of the barge engine was comforting. When the pink cliffs loomed ahead, Sarah stopped and turned to what she called the corridor, a deep, weathered crack in the wall, slightly wider than a person's outstretched arms. Gravel and debris formed a steep slope to the top of the cliffs. She had been through the corridor many times. Twice she had spotted rattlesnakes sunning on loose slabs of limestone. She had tossed rocks until they disappeared into the rubble. She warned Ryan.

"Yes, this looks like a good place for them." He turned, stepped to the edge of the shelf and gazed down at the water. Sarah joined him. This was the end of the cove, a hundred-yard-wide basin of iridescent green contained by smooth, pink limestone.

"Looks inviting, doesn't it?" She had thought that every time she had been here. "Like someone's huge private pool."

"A long swim to get out of this pool," Ryan commented, studying the smooth cliffs.

"Yes," she said, "almost all the way back to the boat, with hardly a handhold in between." She glanced at the boat nosed into the gravel two hundred yards away. "Could you make it?"

Ryan shook his head and appeared thoughtful. "Probably. I swim laps pretty regularly. How about you?"

"I know I can. I swim laps regularly also... right down there."

Ryan looked surprised.

"I have a snorkel and mask on the boat. I have been over this cove dozens of times. It is only ten or twelve feet deep. Fuentes is right – the big sailboat isn't here.

"You're swimming here in the middle of nowhere alone?"

"Only every other day or so lately, but for days at a time when Laura's cap turned up here."

Ryan was silent, staring at her for a moment. "That is pretty amazing," he finally said, "just pretty amazing." He nodded his head, smiled and winked.

Sarah felt her mood change. She took a deep breath, looked down at the water, then without looking up asked, "Is something wrong with your eye? Why do you keep doing that – winking? It looks... silly."

"Nothing wrong with my eye," she heard him reply quietly. "I have a good reason for winking, but if it bothers you, I'll stop."

Sarah looked up at him.

He turned, looked along the shelf for a moment, then stepped back the way they had come and stripped a dry root the size of a broom handle from the cliff wall. "This will take care of any snakes."

"Why were you winking?" Who said that? These were not her words. She was only listening, listening to someone make a fool of herself.

"What?" He turned toward her, the hint of a smile on his lips, but the blue-green eyes were dancing, laughing.

"I asked why you were winking." There, damn it, he had made her ask twice. Maybe she should beg now. Why not? She was already completely ridiculous.

"When I wink, you smile. You didn't realize that?"

"No, I didn't... realize that."

He winked. She felt her face warming, and she smiled.

"See what I mean?"

An air horn blasted from the barge as it made a turn in the basin. Ryan waved to the Mexican Coast Guard. "Let's see where the shots came from." He went into the passageway, striking rocks and matted brush with the root cane. Sarah followed. Surely she hadn't smiled at every stupid wink, she thought.

21

They paused halfway around the end of the cove for Ryan to theorize about Mario's vantage point. He seemed intent and in a hurry until they came to the cenizo-covered mesa. There he slowed, studying the ground. "Fuentes was right about something else. The soldiers were everywhere." She followed him on a sweep into the waist-high sage and back to the slope above the cliffs. "Everything is tromped up. I thought we might backtrack, see where the shooter walked from his boat, but can't tell anything now." He shook his head and followed along the top of the slope above the cliffs, moving back toward the end of the cove. She noticed his glances across the cove. Finally he stopped and stared. "That hill," he pointed across the cove. "That could be where the college student was shot. There's Spanish Dagger halfway down."

Sarah looked across. There were several small hills just back of the cliffs. All had some sort of vegetation on them. She knew desert plants, Spanish Dagger, but not at this distance. What did dagger plants have to do with anything?

"Mario said Patterson slid back down the hill behind some dagger plants after he was shot," Ryan said, as if reading her thoughts. He continued walking for a short distance, then angled into the brush on his left and stopped near a large growth of prickly pear. The ground was reddish, hard-packed sand and gravel. He kicked at it, stared across the cove again and pointed, "I think that must be the place. About a hundred-and-fifty yards. Piece of cake with a scope." He studied it a moment longer then, eyes to the ground; he circled the huge cluster of cactus, pausing on the far side. "Something's been going on here." He squatted, cactus on his right, and surveyed the cove for almost a full minute before standing. "You can cover everything from here." He made a spreading motion with his arms. "See how the cove bends slightly around this point? Like shooting fish in a... sorry."

"All right," she said. The barge had stopped. Sarah watched two divers without tanks go over the side, surface a few seconds later and climb back aboard. The barge resumed its exploration. Sarah turned to Ryan. He was probing the giant prickly pear cluster with his snake stick. She was about to ask what he was doing when a spent cartridge rolled from beneath the bristling green pads. He picked it up and handed it to her. "Thirty-ought-six, months old. Maybe years," he quickly added.

She turned up the shiny side of the half-tarnished casing. "Two months?"

"Probably." He turned and headed for the end of the cove.

"Maybe there are more." She glanced around.

"They were picked up or the soldiers would have found them. That one's too old to interest Fuentes. That leaves the mine. Let's take a quick look before the Coast Guard leaves."

She moved quickly to keep up with him.

♦   ♦   ♦

The line of small hills lay twenty yards inland from the cliffs. As they approached the first one, fossil snails, scattered like gravel along the trail, caught Sarah's eye. Ryan stooped to pick one up. "Bingo," he said, smiling. Sarah smiled back and gathered a handful. They circled the first hill, then the second and third, looking for an opening. In the process, they found that all three hills were made of the same hard, light-gray strata that contained the snails. But where was the hole?

"Out there somewhere?" Sarah faced the barren mesa behind the last hill.

"No," Ryan countered. "It has to be within sight of where we found the shell casing."

And they had already looked within sight of where the casing was found, she thought, as she followed Ryan around the hill to the edge of the cliff.

The Coast Guard boat was stopped, engine idling, under the cliffs across the cove. Everyone seemed to be in the water, no tanks or masks, but plenty of splashing and shouting.

"Our protection." Ryan shook his head. Sarah tossed her handful of snails at the Boston Whaler, forty feet below.

"The hole is filled-in," Ryan said with conviction. "And it's between here and the place we came up from the shelf." He moved away from the cliff and walked slowly toward the corridor. Sarah picked up more snails and tossed them over the cliff. They were everywhere. Strange how she had never noticed them before. She watched the snails hit the water, then hurried to catch up with Ryan.

"Move over about ten yards," he pointed to his right, "and look for a depression, discoloration, anything different about the ground." He didn't look up. She moved over, walking slowly, studying the hard-packed earth. Gray fossil snails everywhere, then she noticed a pink one. Picked it up and looked around. Another one uphill. She turned in that direction and found others. "Pink snails," she called out. Ryan was instantly at her side, and they traced the odd-colored snails to a large area of similarly colored earth near the foot of the second hill. "This is looking good," Ryan said. "Here's a spot that looks loose." He scraped at the small area with his foot. It seemed very loose. He glanced anxiously toward the Coast Guard boat and scraped more gravel. Finally he sat down and pushed away earth with both sneaker soles. "Something is here." As he said it, Sarah saw a flat rusty surface begin to appear.

Ray Summers

22

The iron flange surrounding the manhole cover had been set in concrete. Two rusty handle rings attached to the cover lay across it. Ryan stood and glanced toward the cove, reassuring himself that the Coast Guard boat was out of sight below the rim. He looked back at what they had unearthed, then at Sarah. She nodded. Ryan grasped the iron ring nearest him and tugged. The heavy cover lifted but slid only a few inches over the flange. Sarah grabbed the other ring, and together they heaved the iron cover to one side.

The walkie-talkie on the ground at Ryan's feet began to crackle. He retrieved it and turned the squelch button attempting to tune out the static. "Shaw to any Del Rio unit." He looked down at the top three rungs of a rusty ladder. Below that was only blackness. He called on the radio twice more and concluded that low batteries were causing the static. He turned the radio off.

Sarah dropped a rock into the hole. A few seconds later, it struck something. "I have flashlights in the boat."

"Let's get them. And some rope. That ladder looks old."

♦   ♦   ♦

The ladder was old but sturdy. It reminded him of the iron-strap-and-oversize-rivet construction he had noticed in old jail cells. The nylon rope dangling beside him would not be needed. His right foot touched the cave floor and he stepped off the ladder. He was now forty feet down in a narrow vertical crack that had been skillfully sealed over. He had paused a few feet down the ladder and admired the work. Large slabs of stone, expertly arranged in tiers, spanned a lengthy, four-foot-wide section of the fissure. From there, the original opening narrowed quickly in either direction and, except for the concreted flange holding the cover, was sealed with large single stones. The sealed fissure had then been covered with gravel and rock from the surrounding area to blend with the surface. The work had been done long ago with great care and skill.

Ryan unfastened the battery lantern from his belt and panned the area. The wall opposite the ladder had angled away as he descended and was now ten feet away. To his right, the two walls converged some fifty feet away. To the left, the floor sloped downward, the fissure continuing into the darkness.

"Have you reached the bottom?" Sarah's voice seemed farther than forty or fifty feet away.

"Come on down." This wasn't a good idea, both of them inside at the same time, but the ladder was solid and the Mexican Coast Guard was still frolicking across the cove. He pointed the lantern upward and watched her descent. By the time she was halfway down, he was certain she could make a fortune modeling jeans.

"Hey, you're blinding me."

He lowered the beam. A minute later she stepped off the ladder.

"I wish we had more rope," he said, aiming the lantern down the sloping passageway. "If it gets any steeper, we'll turn back."

"Have you seen this?" She played the beam of her small pocket light across the angled wall. The imbedded petrified snails gave the limestone a peanut-brittle texture; only this peanut brittle was dark, stained by whatever dissolving mineral caused the black streaks on the canyon walls. They were looking at black snails. "I'm going to find out what's down here. This is not going to be one of those 'we almost found it' treasure stories." She started down the slope.

"Here, take the big light."

She turned, giving Ryan a questioning look.

"I'll be right behind you," he said. "Unless it gets steeper, then I'll come back for the rope." They traded lights, and he followed her.

A hundred feet from the ladder, the ground leveled off. The crack widened, made a sharp bend to the right and ended at a clear, quietly moving stream of water. The beam from Sarah's lantern moved quickly to the right along the water to a large hollow in the wall where the stream entered the cavern. The lantern beam darted to the opposite wall twenty-five feet away. Another hollowed area marked the stream's exit.

"This is what we needed," Ryan said, playing the small light around the cave. "Fuentes is going to have a field day when he sees this." An ancient pick-ax and shovel appeared in Ryan's small circle of light, then a modern shovel and a plastic bucket. Ryan glanced up. Sarah had her light on a rusted lantern hanging from the wall.

"That's been here awhile," she said, moving the light along the wall to reveal two more ancient lanterns.

"The bucket and shovel are recent," Ryan said, "and look at this." His light had found a large round shallow pan, leaned edge-up on a small ledge. "Someone's been panning for gold. This really is a gold mine."

Sarah took the pan, stepped to the water and looked down. "Do you know how to pan for gold?"

"No. I'm not sure what gold would look like in a pan full of gravel and sand."

"Me either."

"Let's go find Fuentes."

♦ ♦ ♦

Ryan heard the throb of the large engine moments before Sarah stuck her head back into the opening and shouted that the Coast Guard boat was leaving. Ryan emerged from the cave and joined Sarah at the edge of the cliff. They watched the big barge make a final turn in the basin and plow past them, gathering speed as it headed for the main channel. Ryan glanced across the cove. The large cluster of prickly pear cactus was a gray blur at this distance. "Help me with the cover," he said.

Ryan retrieved the ropes that had been stripped from the Boston Whaler, and the iron cover was moved back into place.

Sarah dropped to the ground and began pushing sand and gravel with her feet. She was smiling.

"Having a good day, I take it," Ryan said as he scooped dry earth over the cover with the side of his foot.

"The best," she looked up at him, "the very best. This is something that cannot be dismissed or ignored. Someone's going to have to investigate." She paused, staring at him, got to her feet, still staring, and said, "Thank you very much." Her voice and eyes said more than thank you.

Ryan moved close to her. "You're quite welcome." He looked down into her blue, unwavering eyes and the atmosphere electrified. He should take her in his arms now. Every tingling nerve in his body said so. Her eyes and lips said so, but a voice had begun to whisper that they should be getting out of there, a voice he had learned to heed. "How far is it to the canyons Fuentes was going to search?" He put an arm around Sarah's shoulders and escorted her toward the corridor. "An hour from here." Her voice sounded weak. They had shaken each other pretty good.

Sarah cleared her throat. "We should trailer the boat and drive to the Mexican marina," she said. "Put the boat back in there. We'll still be an hour from where Fuentes has them searching, but we'll be a lot closer to home after we find him."

"Sounds good."

They walked quietly the remaining distance to the corridor. Standing before the enclosed slope, Ryan shifted the coil of rope to his left shoulder and stooped to pick up his snake-chasing stick. Rocks in the embankment behind them exploded. Ryan spun without straightening, scooped Sarah with his right arm and pushed her into the chasm ahead of him. The sound of the rifle shot reverberated through the cove.

23

Ryan pressed Sarah against the wall and shook the coiled rope from his shoulder. The crevasse angled slightly into the cliff walls, enough to put them out of the line of fire until the sniper changed positions. Ryan looked down the slope. The right wall bulged inward near the bottom. "He'll be lined up on us any minute. Let's try for the outcrop near the entrance."

"I'm right behind you."

He felt the vibration of her voice, glanced over and saw that his right hand was in the center of her chest, pinning her against the wall. "Stay close." He released her, turned and charged down the rock-littered slope. His agility surprised him, his feet finding mostly solid footing down thirty yards of sharp rubble. He thought he could hear Sarah a step behind.

A bullet whined from the rocks to the rear as Ryan smashed into the limestone protrusion. An instant later, Sarah slammed into his back. He turned and pulled her in front of him into the corner. "You all right?"

"Yes."

He turned, staring up the slope. "We're in good shape here until he comes for us." Ryan was remembering the view from the other side of the cove, how everything could be covered: the cliff tops, the shelf, water, all wide open. They were in the only cover, but that wouldn't last. He leaned out for a look at the cove, ducking back an instant before the rock in front of him exploded.

"Don't do that again," Sarah said, squirming deeper into the corner.

"I'm thinking of something pretty crazy," Ryan said.

"Let's hear it. You're doing pretty good so far."

Her voice sounded muffled. He looked over. She had her head

down, face buried in folded arms.

"He's gong to kill us if we stay here," Ryan said, softly.

"What's the idea?"

"From his position, it's twenty yards to the edge of the cliff. Even if he has a semi-automatic, it will take a couple of seconds for him to get back on target after firing, especially if he's using a scope – and I'm pretty sure he is."

Sarah's voice was still muffled by folded arms. "OK, you stick your head out again, he shoots, we run, make it into the water. Then what? He gets to shoot fish in a barrel?"

Her mind was quick, he thought. "Can you make it across the cove underwater?"

She looked up, shook her head. "That's way too far on one breath, got to be a hundred yards at least."

"It would be less than that. The slope above the cliff has him set pretty far back and I didn't see a way down when we were over there. We could be out of his line of fire three quarters of the way across."

They both knew it was still too far on one breath.

Sarah stared at him. "We make the other side, a sheer rock wall and…." She was still staring.

"I'm working on that. I'm going to have another look, keep him busy. If he moves to the end of the cove, he'll have all the water surface covered." Before Sarah could object, he stuck his head out. This time the limestone shattered in front of his face as he pulled back.

"Damn, I told you not to do that again," Sarah said.

Ryan coughed, shook his head, and brushed chips from the left side of his face. He heard Sarah catch her breath. He looked over. She had a shocked look on her face. "What?" Then he saw blood on his left hand. He stared as if it belonged to someone else. He raised it to his ear and found a large cut near the tip. "Rock cut." He wiped the bloody hand on his jeans and glanced at the blood on his shoulder. They were quiet for a moment. Ryan felt at his ear again.

"Let's go for it," Sarah said. "Try for the other side. I know where there might be an opening in the cliff.

"A cave?"

"A crack. Until the lake came up last month it was full of wild bees. The lower part was wide and deep enough to hide in but it may be underwater now."

"The bees are gone?"

"They moved out when the water got high."

"All right, we try for the bee cave." He heard himself agreeing to a suicide pact. It was all they had. "Strip." He leaned over, pulling at his sneaker laces.

"What?"

"You won't get far weighted down with wet clothes. Strip 'em off."

She hesitated a moment, then threw her hat onto the rocks and yanked the T-shirt off over her head. The bra was powder blue. Sneakers came off next, then a quick, short struggle with the tight jeans. Her blue panties matched the bra.

Ryan was down to green jockeys. He rolled their discarded clothing into a long bundle, pulling his hat over one end of the roll.

"Ready?"

"Ready," she said, looking up at him. "Thanks for everything."

He nodded, looked into her eyes for a moment then said, "Let's breathe." They inhaled and exhaled deeply until she nodded. He pushed the clothing around the outcrop. "When we clear the corridor, angle left. I'll go right. See you on the other...." A bullet ripped the clothing from his hands.

Ray Summers

24

The sniper smiled. Of course it was only a stuffed hat. They were up to something. "I'll bite," he said aloud. "You're not going anywhere." He squeezed the trigger. The recoil of the M-1 rocked him gently backward. He loved that feeling, and the rifle. Its gas-operated system and notorious heavy weight minimized recoil, allowing the offset scope to be quickly brought back on target. In this instance, there was no hurry. They were trapped. He might give them another lesson or two, show them they couldn't expose a fingernail without losing it, then he would stroll to the other side and... what was that? Two figures bolting out of the crevasse, separating, streaking across the shelf. He shifted left, squeezed off a round, but the almost-naked man was already off the shelf, headfirst into the lake. The rifle came back down, but there were no targets. He lowered the rifle, stood and looked toward their boat. It was more than a hundred yards east of the crevasse and was being moved in his direction by a light breeze. He had seen it lifted off the beach by the heavy wake of the departing Mexican Coast Guard barge. Forgot to tie up, he had thought. He sat back down, braced his elbows into his knees as he brought the rifle to his shoulder and waited for them to surface. It was so stupid of them to try for the boat. He was good at turtle and garfish shooting.

The man surfaced first, far left of where the rifle was pointed. The sniper swung and fired, knowing he was too late. Then the woman broke the surface and disappeared as he found her in the scope and fired. He lowered the rifle and stared. No bubbles, no bloody foam, but he knew their intent now, should have guessed it. Swimming under the cliff, out of the line of fire, for all the good that would do them. He stood, slung the rifle and started toward the end of the cove. There was no safe way down the steep slope to reach the edge of the cliff in front of him, but it was only a few minutes to the other side. Then he would end it. He had never been put to this much trouble before. He shouldn't have allowed them to reach the crevasse, but he had expected them to stop any second, embrace and kiss, as they almost had at the mine entrance. Then he would have taken them both with one shot. It would have been his first double.

He paused at the end of the cove, a clear view under the pink cliffs now before him. No movement, hardly even wave action this far from the main channel. He waited, watchful for several minutes, then moved on, looking now for a cave, a niche, anyplace they could be hiding. At the crevasse, he paused, stepped inside, glanced at the scattered clothing. Blood on the man's shirt, a neck or head wound. Something serious he hoped. Smiling, he left the crevasse and continued slowly along the shelf. Fifty yards east of the crevasse, he paused, raised the rifle and peered through the scope. Smooth pink limestone, hardly a nick in its surface, flowed past the lens as he scanned the cliff across the cove at water level, first to the end of the cove, then back, to the point directly across, where he had begun, and on eastward.

Suddenly, he stopped and moved the scope slowly back over the area just covered. He had almost passed it by, a crack less than a foot wide. He traced it to the top of the cliff, then brought the scope back to water level and stared. Too small, or so it appeared from this angle. He lowered the rifle, walked another twenty yards and raised the rifle again. The crack was directly across from him. Too small, unless it was wider inside. He nestled the rifle butt into his shoulder, flipped the safety tab forward with his trigger finger and fired three quick shots. Powdered stone curled from the opening like cigarette smoke. He noted with satisfaction that the surface of the cliff remained unmarked. All three shots had gone cleanly into the narrow fracture. He moved the scope slowly eastward another fifty yards, much farther than they could possibly have covered in such short time, lowered the rifle and again surveyed the cove with his naked eye. Nothing, only the drifting boat now to his left near the middle of the cove. Maybe he had tagged both of them when they surfaced for air. He found a place to sit and lean back against the cliff. If they weren't in the crack, they were dead, but something was telling him to wait.

Ray Summers

25

The first shot sent chips flying inside the chamber. Sarah heard Ryan say, "Down," and they submerged together. The next two shots were dull hammer blows against stone. She felt his hands on her bare back. She raised her arms in front of her, pushed against the slick wall, and they were anchored underwater in the oblong chimney. This was the position they had devised a few minutes earlier on the surface inside the chimney, an alternative to treading water. Sarah opened her eyes to the gray mass directly in front of her. A few inches to the left was a strip of green haze, the opening that had been such a disappointment from the outside. She had thrust her fingers into the six-inch-wide crack and pulled, as if she could spread it. Ryan had discovered the wide opening below with his feet, signaled her, and they had gone down together. She entered the chimney first as he held her right ankle. Seconds later, he surfaced beside her, wiping water from his face, glancing around inside the lopsided stone chimney with a crack running down one side. "We made it," she'd said, and winked at him. He had smiled.

Now she relaxed the pressure against her side of the chamber and they rose to the surface. The acrid scent of burnt stone greeted them. She turned, her eye catching the three white spatters in the rose-colored stone to the right of Ryan's head. He had suggested hugging the chimney's elongated side. It had kept them a few inches away from the line of fire. "All three just above water level," he whispered, "and you could cover them with a coffee cup. He's got a scope, all right."

They turned away from the bullet scars, treading water, expecting more shots, ready to submerge again. When no more bullets came they returned to anchor position. A few minutes later, they altered the position, making it back-to-back.

"That's better," Sarah said, "warmer. Are you cold?"

"I don't want to think about it," he answered. "It's a long time until dark."

"He'll have to go for his boat," Sarah said. "If we knew when, we could swim for the Whaler."

"I hate to bring this up, but there may be more than one person."

She was silent. She hadn't thought of that.

"I don't think we can count on the Whaler. He'll either pick it up or be watching it. Any other ideas?"

"Chango's," she answered immediately. "Chango's place is only a mile south." But Chango had lied about the snails, she thought.

Ryan put his suspicions in more direct terms. "Chango may be the one trying to kill us."

Sarah was quiet for a moment, then whispered, "Seminole Canyon – two miles north. The fenced-off rock paintings there in Panther Cave are protected by an alarm system."

"That's it," Ryan said. "Trip the alarm and wait for the rangers. That's good."

Two miles in the dark, Sarah thought, no shoes, no clothes, another swim, and a ten-foot fence topped with razor wire. You are in real trouble when that is "good."

♦ ♦ ♦

The sound of the first bump stiffened them. Sarah's eyes sprang open. Light from the crack was dim, darkness coming at last – darkness and something else? The second bump was followed by a scraping sound. She was frozen, back-to-back with Ryan, feet braced against the wall in front, staring at the crack, expecting a probing boat hook, or more shots. Another bump, closer. The chimney darkened; something nudged the crack and then moved on. The pressure on her back eased and she was afloat. She turned. Ryan was gone. But, he hadn't signaled. She made a sweep for him with her feet. She was alone. Where was he?

"It's our boat." The whispered voice startled her. She spun, staring at the dim crack. Our boat? The bumping and scraping was the Whaler?

"Can you hear me?"

"Yes."

"It's almost dark. When I get the motor started, come on out."

She took a deep breath, submerged and came up beside him.

"When the motor starts, we'll be in that boat together."

She stared past him at the Boston Whaler a few feet away, nosing its way along the cliff. The shelf across the cove was a gray strip. Clouds overhead still held a tinge of pink.

"Let's do it." Ryan pushed off, breast-stroking toward the Whaler.

Sarah followed, pulling silently through the water, wondering if rifle telescopes worked as well as binoculars in dim light.

The side of the Whaler seemed six feet high as she came alongside. The stern, weighted by the motor was slightly lower. Ryan tried hoisting himself aboard, but there was no grip, only smooth Fiberglass. She was watching him study the situation when she heard the sound of a distant outboard. She turned toward it. A boat in the main channel?

"Come here." Ryan was no longer whispering. His tone told her that he also heard the motor. She closed the short distance between them. He had found a hold on the raised motor and was dangling, face to transom, by his outstretched left arm. "Put your foot in my hand." She did as he said and was raised high enough to lean into the boat. As she groped for a handhold, an open hand pressed her buttocks, lifting and dumping her onto the deck.

"Lower the motor," he said.

She moved to the bow, retrieved the ignition key from its storage-bin hiding place. The drone of outboard had grown louder. The sniper was coming for the Whaler. She hurried to the console, inserted the key and turned it. "Coming down," she said, flipping the switch and stepping to the stern. Ryan eased up alongside the lowered motor, putting a hand on the stern. "Got a foot on the..." He slipped, feet-first, back into the water. "...hydroplane," he said, surfacing. He moved up the outboard again, this time leaning into the boat and moving his right leg over the stern. Sarah grabbed the foot and pulled him aboard.

"Let's get the hell out of here." He was on his feet, moving toward the bow. Sarah started the motor and backed away from the cliff. As she headed out of the cove, Ryan tossed the rifle case aside and positioned himself in the bow. Beyond, there was only darkness. She maneuvered to the middle of the cove and pushed the throttle forward, navigating by the cliffs' silhouettes on either side. The whine of the approaching outboard could no longer be heard above the sound of the Whaler's eighty-five horsepower. Ahead in the darkness, red dots flashed, and then the sound of shots reached her. Something thudded against the boat. On his knees in the bow, Ryan opened fire. Something struck her forehead, then her left shoulder. She crouched behind the steering console, examining her shoulder, crying out as something hot landed on her bare back. It rolled onto the deck against her foot. She kicked it away.

"Are you hit?" Ryan was beside her, rifle in hand, bandolier dangling from his neck.

"No, it was just a hot casing."

The sound of more shots, much nearer now, came from the darkness ahead. "I can't see him," Ryan said, shoving more ammunition into the rifle. "Only muzzle flashes." He stood and began firing. "He's dead ahead."

Sarah straightened enough to reach the throttle, shoved it completely forward and leaned over the steering wheel. She hoped the Whaler would take the bastard head-on. As she finished that thought, the bow of the Whaler snapped to the right. Ryan went to his knees, and onto the deck as something ripped along the port side. Sarah looked back, saw only the Whaler's glistening wake. Facing forward again, she glanced around for Ryan, wondering if he would be angry that she had rammed the other boat and dumped him. He sat up a few feet away, picked up the rifle, jacked two shells from it, laid it back on the deck, removed the bandolier from around his neck and dropped it onto the rifle. "Could you slow this thing down? I'm freezing."

She slowed the boat to cruising speed, staring at the black wall taking shape ahead. She was cold also, shaking, teeth chattering. She had been cold in the water for hours, but this was unbearable. The bra and panties were nothing against the cutting wind. Her mind ran through the Whaler's storage compartments, no jacket, blanket, or sleeping bag, only a light plastic rain slicker in the starboard bin. "Raincoat," she chattered, pointing.

She made the swing left into the main channel as Ryan shook the slicker open and came toward her. "Put it on," she said.

"I'm all right," he said, shivering and raised the plastic to slip it over her head.

Put it on and take the wheel. I'll get in behind you."

He seemed to nod, pulled the slicker's neck opening over his head, and took her place behind the steering console.

She moved behind him, raised the plastic and slipped under. He flinched when the side of her face touched his back. She put both arms around him, pulled herself close, felt him stiffen and take a deep breath. He was like a block of ice. She probably felt the same to him. She squeezed tighter, pushed the blue panties against him. He pushed back. Her hands moved down to the green jockeys. They would be warm soon.

Ray Summers

26

The sniper's first concern was the rifle. He held it barrel-down along his left side and with his free arm stroked toward the capsized jonboat. They had caught him almost head-on as he reloaded, the crazy bastards. Where had they been? Inside the crack? He would check on that when things were back under control. Crazy bastards. No one had ever escaped before. Everything had been considered except stripping, swimming, disappearing and having a drifting boat handy. Now he would have to improvise, follow them into town, get them quickly... tonight.

His fishing boat was bottom side up, motor shaft and propeller protruding skyward. The sealed compartments under the seats kept it afloat. He had contributed to the upset by swerving as he lunged overboard away from the looming white bow. Crazy bastards. Three rounds had hit the jonboat. Another parted his hair. He pressed his right shoulder against the overturned metal boat, slipped his left arm into the rifle sling, turned and worked his way along the boat to the square bow. He grasped the metal handhold and stroked for shore. Sarah hadn't been in the Winnebago for the last two nights. Shacking up with her new boat buddy, probably. The motel listing for Del Rio was short, less than one yellow page. He had gone through the list last night telephoning for Sarah. It would take only a few minutes to do the same for Mr. Shaw.

♦   ♦   ♦

Ryan opened his eyes and stared at the dim outline of a strange window. He pulled the warm sheet and blanket tighter around his neck. God, he had been cold inside that stone chimney... and on the boat. He half-sat, supporting himself on one elbow, and stared down at Sarah's short curly hair. So it wasn't a dream. They really had gone at each other like that... in the bed bay of the Ranchero, here on the bed, the shower.... He moved closer to her, chest against her back. She had awakened him earlier during the night. Turnabout was fair play, he thought, and kissed the back of her neck until she turned toward him.

◆   ◆   ◆

The sniper sat in darkness, back against the passenger door of his pickup, legs extended on the seat in front of him. The door to Ryan Shaw's motel room was fifty yards away. The scoped .22 rifle lay under a blanket on the floorboard. Unlike his old large-caliber military rifle, the light semi-automatic had no recoil. He could move instantly from one target to another. Noise from the nearby refrigerator trucks would cover the negligible sound of the shots. At this close range, neck shots would do the trick, drop them like a couple of white-tailed deer yearlings if they came out together. He hoped they would come out together.

A shadow crossed the lighted corridor leading to the rear door of the motel office. A figure crossed the lighted pool area, then in front of Shaw's room, and came toward the rear parking lot. The sniper sat perfectly still as the man crunched toward him across the unpaved lot then veered off to one of the eighteen-wheelers. A moment later, a diesel engine chugged to life. When it was running smoothly, a door slammed and the driver was back on the ground. The sniper watched as the rig's tires and air hoses were checked with a flashlight. Suddenly, there was a rap on the window behind him. Startled, he leaned forward, looked back, and was blinded with a bright light in his face.

"You all right?" The voice outside the window was muffled.

The sniper shielded his eyes with one hand, cracked the window with the other. "Yes, I'm fine."

The light played around the interior of the pickup cab, paused for a moment on the blanket covering the rifle, then went out. "Sorry, didn't know it was you."

The sniper blinked and squinted, and the security guard came into focus. It was a man he knew. "Rough night," the sniper explained. "Thought I would get some breakfast before heading home."

"Boy, you look like something the cat dragged in." The guard chuckled, shaking his head, and turned the light onto his watch. "About fifteen minutes until the buffet opens. I've got another round to make over at the Holiday Inn then I'll join you." He rapped the top of the pickup with his knuckles and walked away.

The sniper waited until he saw the little blue car with a stick-on red roof light pull away from the front of the motel before moving to the driver's side of his pickup. He started the engine and drove toward the highway. He had simply leaned over in the pickup, out of sight, every time the old retired deputy made a pass in his ancient blue Chevy Malibu. Foot patrol by the security guard had not been anticipated. The guard would remember. It was over for now. He had never made this many mistakes before. The sniper pulled onto the highway and drove toward town. Betty's Ranch House would already be open for breakfast.

27

Ryan opened the front door to the Customs Agents Office and stepped in. Jean Harris was seated behind her desk. The IA agent from Houston stood up from a nearby chair.

"We need to talk," Ochoa said, then turned and strode down the hall. Jean raised her eyebrows. Ryan smiled and followed Ochoa. Seeing the IA agent's blue Corvette parked out front was the first thought he had given to Fred Ochoa since leaving the office almost 24 hours ago. What were his departing words to Ochoa? Read the statements and give me a call... something like that. But then he hadn't been back to his motel room until early morning.

"Just what the hell is going on?" Ochoa was in front of their now-shared borrowed desk, arms folded, head cocked to one side. "I'm told to drop everything, that this is hot, top priority. I bust my ass, drive half the night getting here, and you toss a stack of papers at me and split. I called your room until midnight last night, then checked with the RAC to see if we should start a search party. He says no, that you've been sniffing around one of the female witnesses and were probably shacked-up with her."

Ryan blinked. Everything Ochoa had just said was absolutely true. "I'm sorry. I was just not able to call you last night." He stepped behind the desk and sat down. "Now tell me what else is bothering you. You were pissed off yesterday when we first met."

Ochoa was still standing, arms folded. His dark eyes locked on Ryan's. "That's right. I was pissed. I'm still pissed, and I'm going to be pissed until this is over." He began nodding his head. "This was my case. We've been hearing things about Banner for quite some time, but there were no actual complaints, no witnesses. Finally, that memo from the

Immigration inspector was exactly what we needed to open an investigation, which we did. A few phone calls convinced me that there would probably be no witnesses, so I came up with a plan to catch him. Then headquarters gets into it and you show up asking questions and blow the whole plan. Nobody checked with IA first. Now we'll never get him."

"What exactly did I mess up?"

"Just a damn good sting, a female agent from Los Angeles lined up to come here undercover, cross back and forth until he tried to take her clothes off. But that's out now. You alerted him."

Ryan considered what Ochoa had said and sympathized. He knew first-hand the talent, or maybe better lack of it, that caused headquarters to screw up ongoing investigations. Then he recalled the question he'd had when he first received the file from Immigration. "The Immigration memo is dated three months ago. "How long does it take a female agent to get from Los Angeles to Texas?"

"She was undercover on another deal, finished up last week, and would have been in my office in Houston on Monday."

"Allowing for paper flow, that's still over two months. You couldn't come up with another female agent?"

"Possibly, but this one had... qualifications. Banner would have done anything to get her into the search room." Ochoa raised his hands in front of his chest and stifled a grin.

"Sounds like entrapment." Ryan said and leaned over to cover his own smile. "I apologize again for last night. Ruining your plan wasn't my fault." He explained the Senator Cowden connection. "I thought his grandkids were lying, making it all up. I thought they had been caught with pills or something and were trying to cover themselves. I was not unhappy at the chance to bail everybody out of what seemed a bad situation." Ryan paused, eyes locked with Ochoa's. "Didn't turn out that way and when I'm done with this, I'll be opening another investigation to find out who did the sloppy background investigation on this creep."

Ochoa's glare softened. "I'll save you that trouble. I did his background investigation."

Ryan was stunned. "How...?"

Ochoa interrupted. "September a year ago, you know the drill: Hold new positions vacant for a year, spend the money allotted for them elsewhere until the last minute, then fill all vacant positions so they won't be lost. I made phone calls, wrote memos trying to keep this guy off the rolls. I knew an ATF agent in his office. The candidate originally lined up for our vacancy got tired of the runaround and went to the Coast Guard. Banner had his application in, was already a Treasury agent in ATF, so they grabbed him, almost overnight, to keep from losing the position. I did his official background investigation two damned weeks after he was hired."

Ryan nodded. He understood perfectly well why Fred Ochoa was... pissed. "Inspector Banner seems to have incredible luck. Let's change it. We have five witnesses...." The telephone interrupted. Ryan picked it up. It was Jean.

"There's a woman here who doesn't speak English. Someone in a black Mercedes dropped her off. I think she's looking for you."

♦   ♦   ♦

Ryan ushered the Mexican woman into the borrowed office. She was tall, slender with large dark eyes. "Fred, this is Elvia Arispe-Lorenzo," he said in Spanish, "The woman who works for Mexican Immigration."

Ochoa smiled nodded and offered her a chair. Ryan sat down beside her in front of the desk. Ochoa took a seat next to the wall.

"We would like to ask you some questions about Inspector Banner." Ryan noticed her eyes widen. "We know you have been seeing him."

Her eyes widened more like a frightened animal's, then focused on the floor in front of her.

"If you are doing so willingly, it is none of our business. But if he is somehow forcing himself on you we would like to know about it." Ryan glanced at Ochoa. The IA agent was also studying the floor.

"Yes, I know him," the woman said. "I wish I didn't. He said he found pills in my purse, but he didn't. I have never had contraband in my purse. He said he would take my card and tell the people I work for. I have been meeting him every night he works at the dam. I have two babies, my mother and sister to support. I meet him whenever he says."

"You're not going to lose your card," Ryan assured her. He stood and reached for his briefcase on the desk. "Anything you want to ask her while I'm getting set up?" He glanced at Ochoa.

"I guess not," the IA agent answered. "I don't know what's going on. I don't speak Spanish."

Ryan had just opened his silver aluminum briefcase to retrieve his recorder. He turned to Ochoa. "You don't speak Spanish?"

"I don't speak Spanish." Ochoa looked embarrassed and folded his arms.

Ryan shook his head. He had specifically requested a Spanish speaker. He had known one other Hispanic agent who spoke no Spanish. Well... now he knew two. Ryan slapped the recorder onto the desk and looked at the frightened woman. "Are you married?" he asked in Spanish.

"No."

Ryan looked at Ochoa again. "You don't know any Spanish at all?"

"No." The answer was short.

Ryan punched the record button on the recorder and had the woman Identify herself. She answered Ryan's questions willingly, describing her first encounter with Banner, his threats, and the late-night rendezvous that followed. "When he worked at the dam, I had to meet him there almost every night when the office closed. When everyone was gone he would take me up on the roof. Sometimes we were there only an hour or so; sometimes he kept me until dawn."

Ryan turned to Ochoa, who was still sporting a disgruntled look. "Would it surprise you to hear that Banner found a bottle of pills in her purse six months ago?"

Ochoa straightened in his chair as Ryan told him the whole story. "You would think the bastard would vary his M.O. just a little."

"He's taking her up on the roof of the port?"

"It's set up as an observation deck. The Border Patrol uses it for still watch sometimes during the day. If the weather is nice, the inspectors eat lunch up there."

"She's been meeting him for six months? If she's afraid of losing her job, why is she talking to us?"

"Good point." Ryan posed the question to Elvia.

Elvia Arispe-Lorenzo glanced back and forth at the two agents. "Last week he checked my sister's card and saw that she was related to me. Now he wants me to bring her next time I meet him. My sister is only twelve years old."

Ryan stared at her. The price of keeping her cleaning and cooking job had gotten too high for Elvia. He found himself thinking about Ochoa's plan to run a female agent at Banner.

"There is something more."

Ryan nodded for her to continue.

"Sunday night, the last time I was with him, we watched the Mayor's sailboat sink."

"What?"

"It was very late," Elvia continued. "I heard a motor. I have heard boats pass there before but never so late, and this one sounded different. I sat up and looked but could see nothing, no boat lights, nothing. Passing boats always have lights. This time, I could just hear the sound of a big motor passing, but the sound never completely faded. Soon I could hear that it was returning. It was a big sailboat and it stopped just beyond the lights of the dam. I woke Banner, and we watched it for a few minutes. Then he pulled me back onto the blanket. Later I heard a different motor and looked again. The big boat was sinking. I couldn't see the other boat, but I heard it leaving. I told Banner. As we watched, there was the sound of a crash out on the lake. and the motor sound stopped. Banner laughed and said the departing boat had hit something. Then the sailboat sunk. Banner said someone was going to collect the insurance. The next day Banner came to my house. He said the boat belonged to the mayor and we should say nothing about what we had seen."

"The other boat hit something?" Ryan asked.

"That's what Banner said, and that's the way it sounded."

The island, that all-but-submerged island the Mexican Coast Guard boat had grounded on Thursday morning. Ryan pulled the small notebook from his coat pocket as he stood, opened it as he moved around the desk, picked up the phone and punched in one of his recently added numbers.

"Paulson's Boat and Motor," a rough voice answered.

"Greg, this is Ryan Shaw. Sorry to bother you, but I need to know whose boat you took off the island Monday morning."

"Chango's," came the expected answer. "He ran it up high and dry."

"That seems a little unusual for someone familiar with the lake. Had he been drinking?"

"Maybe, but he was OK by the time I met him at the marina around nine. He spent the night on the island, flagged down a couple of bass fishermen. They brought him in."

Ryan didn't wait for questions. "Thanks. By the way, that's my white Dodge in front of your office. I'll pick it up later if it's not in the way." Paulson said the car was OK. Ryan broke the connection and pressed Jean's number. After dropping him off, Sarah had headed for the Mexican marina to contact Fuentes. Now there was more than the lost gold mine and ambush to tell him about. When jean answered, Ryan asked her to get the Mexican marina on the line for him. Replacing the phone, he turned to Ochoa. "I guess you heard about the missing mayor."

"Yes."

"Command post for the search has been set up at the Mexican marina."

Ochoa stared blankly. Ryan stared back for a moment, then remembered. Of course, the Hispanic who knew no Spanish would have no idea that the Mexican woman had just told them where the mayor's sailboat was. Ryan straightened in the chair and brought the IA agent up to date, adding, "It's something I got involved in, and there's even more. We'll talk about it later, but right now...." He turned his attention to the Mexican woman. "I think she'll wear a wire for us. What can we do with that?"

"Prove Banner is forcing the meetings on her, if she can get him to admit it on tape."

The phone rang. Ryan picked it up. Jean had the marina on the line.

Ryan spoke in Spanish, asking for Fuentes, then Sarah, switching to English when she came on the line. "The Mayor's boat was sunk in front of the dam early Sunday morning." He tried to speak slowly and matter-of-factly.

"In front of the dam? How do you know that?"

"Someone who saw it go down just told me. I'll explain later. Has Fuentes been there?"

"He's expected any minute."

"Tell him where the boat is, but don't tell him Chango sunk it." He could imagine the stunned look on her face.

"What?"

"Remember Paulson saying he pulled a boat off the submerged island Monday morning?" He didn't wait for her answer. "It was Chango's. He ran it aground after sinking the sailboat. He was the one trying to kill us yesterday." He paused. There was silence on the other end. "Just tell Fuentes someone saw the boat go down and called the office. We need to think about Chango." Sarah agreed.

Ryan hung up and turned to Ochoa. "Like I said, something I got involved in." He pulled the open brief case toward him, took Banner's work schedule from the cover pocket and glanced at it. "He's on duty. Came to work at eight this morning." He tossed the paper back into the briefcase. "Let's go for the wire, see what she can get out of him."

Ochoa nodded.

Ryan spoke Spanish to Elvia. "We want you to help us prevent Banner from molesting your sister."

◆　　◆　　◆

An hour later Elvia was wired. Ochoa drove her across the bridge to Ciudad Acuña, left her at the bus stop and returned to the Customs Agents' Office. He stood in front of the reception area's large window, binoculars aimed at the port of entry across the street. "Bus is here," he said. Ryan stood beside him. The green-and-yellow Del Rio city bus was clearly visible to the naked eye. They had been listening to the radio receiver as Elvia conversed with other passengers. Ochoa had instructed her to talk, even to herself if necessary, so adjustments could be made on the recording equipment. Ochoa lowered the binoculars, stepped to the open case of recording equipment atop Jean's desk and lowered the volume. Voices had grown louder and clearer on the small speaker as the bus approached. Ochoa depressed control buttons, studied the surveillance kit for a moment, and then announced, "Everything's on tape from now on."

Ryan continued staring out the window. Earlier, he'd had to confess he was not familiar with the latest electronic equipment borrowed from the Del Rio RAC's office. Ochoa knew all about it and had assumed technical duties. Score a big one for the IA agent.

A tired voice grew louder on the speaker, repeating the same questions over and over in Spanish; "What is your citizenship? What are you bringing from Mexico?" Elvia was approaching the inspector on pedestrian-lane duty. Ryan could now see the first of the passengers streaming from the port building and reboarding the bus. Elvia's voice answered the inspector's rote questions and asked for Banner. "Inside," the tired voice said.

"Thank you," Elvia answered meekly.

A gray Impala suddenly pulled up in front of the window. Ryan took a step back, still peering through the half-opened blinds. Gordon Shanks was the driver, microphone in hand, talking on the car radio. Loud static erupted from the equipment speaker behind him. Ryan half turned, glancing at Ochoa, then the crackling surveillance kit.

"That's interference from the car radio out front," Ryan said. "I'll take care of it." He hurried to the front door, threw it open and ran the few steps to Gordon's car. This had happened to him before, years ago, radio transmissions from a nearby car disrupting reception from a weaker body transmitter. Ryan circled the rear of the Impala and yanked open the driver's door. Gordon looked surprised.

"We've got something going here." Ryan glanced toward the port. "We need for you to move to the back of the building and stay off the radio."

Gordon blinked at him, said OK, and lowered the microphone. Ryan eased the car door closed and hurried back into the building.

"He told her to meet him outside," Ochoa said as Ryan closed the front door behind him. "There she is," Jean said excitedly, staring through the blinds. Ryan returned to his place at the window. The large, paved, unfenced lot on the north side of the port of entry was utilized primarily for Customs inspection of commercial trucks laden with Mexican merchandise. This morning the area was deserted.

Elvia waited alone on the empty loading dock that ran the width of the building. The city bus pulled away from the port. Elvia stared after it. Wishing she were on it, Ryan thought. He heard the rear door open and slam, then footsteps coming up the hall. Ryan glanced over his shoulder as Gordon entered the reception area. The young agent quickly surveyed the scene, eyes lingering on the open electronic surveillance kit.

"Sorry about that," he said, glancing out the window manned by Ryan and Jean.

"No problem," Ryan said. "Bert and Tom were here earlier. Now everyone knows. I didn't want to put it out on the radio."

"Magic Fingers?"

"Right," Ryan answered. "He's coming out to meet the woman on the loading dock any minute now." He nodded toward the window. "And she's wired."

Gordon stepped to the window between Ryan and Jean and also peered out. "Cool, pretty cool. Can I stay?"

"Sure. As a matter of fact, I saw a couple of video cameras in the equipment room. Why don't you run one for us? Might as well have a movie of this, too."

Gordon had the camera loaded and the lens jammed between the blind blades when Banner stepped out of a side door onto the dock. Without so much as a suspicious glance around he strode straight to Elvia.

"So what's going on? You miss me already?" The voice was loud and clear. Gordon had the video camera rolling. Besides being recorded by the surveillance equipment, everything coming over the speaker would also be on the videotape. Ryan reminded everyone that comments made by anyone in the room would be recorded on the video sound track.

"There is a man looking for me, a U.S. federal agent," Elvia said. "He has been to my supervisor. He wants to talk to me about you."

Ryan smiled. That was good, better than they had rehearsed it. If nothing else came of this meeting, Banner was going to be very upset by this revelation.

Ryan looked away from the window at Fred Ochoa hovering over his equipment like a mother hen; Jean's face was glued to the blinds and Gordon had the camera viewfinder crammed into his right eye. If Gordon had arrived a few minutes later, jabbering on his car radio....

Ryan turned back to the window. Banner had begun firing questions at Elvia almost immediately. Now he was leaning slightly forward, toward Elvia, hands gesturing, and mouth spouting orders. Ryan felt his jaw muscles tighten and his mouth slowly stretch into a smile. This was because he could see and hear everything that was going on across the street. He had witnessed others like "Magic Fingers" self-destruct, and it never failed to give him a warm feeling to be even remotely responsible for it.

Ryan savored his moment of contentment. But it was soon overshadowed when the reason for an uneasiness he had been feeling came to him, an uneasiness caused by something that had just occurred and something similar that happened yesterday: static on the walkie-talkie radio when he and Sarah slid the iron cover off the Lost Caracol Mine entrance.

28

Sarah was relieved to see the Boston Whaler. They'd had only the bungee cord and a scrap of rope to tie it to the dock last night. All available line had been stripped from the boat for yesterday's gold-mine exploration.

"It looks low in the water," she remarked as she trailed Ryan down the boat ramp.

"A wonder it didn't break loose," Ryan said over his shoulder, "or sink." He had mentioned several times on the drive out that he heard bullets striking the boat during last night's gunfight. She followed him onto the dock's wooden planking. "About a foot of water in it," he said as they approached the boat. "I told you we took some hits." He leaned over, dropped the long blue canvas bag he was carrying and tugged on the pencil-thin bungee cord.

The Boston Whaler moved sluggishly toward them. Ryan straightened, staring down into the boat. Sarah smiled at an overlooked tag on the new jeans of his second "rough duty" uniform, as he called his second wardrobe purchase in two days, this one replacing the casual wear he was forced to abandon yesterday.

"The bilge pump will take care of the water as soon as we're underway," Sarah said as she leaned over to place her briefcase on the dock. She kicked off her worn white sneakers and rolled up the pant legs of her jeans. Sneakers and briefcase in hand, she stepped down into the flooded boat. The cool water came just above her ankles. She tossed the briefcase and sneakers onto the starboard bench seat as Ryan handed her the blue equipment bag. The big rifle and bandoliers of ammunition inside were heavy. She put the bag on the bench seat beside the briefcase and waded to the steering column. She waited until Ryan replaced the scrap of rope on the Whaler's bow with the new twenty-foot line she had picked up at Paulson's. Then Sarah started the motor.

Ryan removed his new walking shoes, rolled up his pant legs, and stepped aboard. She moved the throttle forward, turned the Whaler away from the dock and headed it downriver. Mexican *federales* and the Coast Guard were to meet them at the cove.

Fuentes had listened attentively as she described the hidden gold mine and the almost-fatal attack on her and Ryan yesterday. When she recounted what Ryan had said about the missing sailboat, Fuentes immediately summoned the Coast Guard, and the huge boat began a methodical sweep in front of the dam. When Ryan arrived at the marina he went over everything again with Fuentes, adding that he believed the mine entrance was wired to a radio alarm system. "Meet us there," Ryan said, "I'll show you how to trap him."

Sarah looked down at the soggy blue carpet and advanced the throttle. Ten minutes of slow running had all but drained the boat. The bow came up and the remaining water drained toward the bilge pump in the stern. She glanced at Ryan. He was squinting ahead, a hand shading his eyes. Except for the sun in his face, he looked comfortable in his new street clothes. She leaned over, unlatched the brief case, took out Laura's faded red cap and handed it to Ryan. "I'll send you a new one when I get home." Home... that disturbing thought again. How could she go back to a boring little gift shop and a cold empty apartment? But go she must... tomorrow, to do battle with the IRS or lose everything.

Ryan tried the hat, adjusted the size, pulled it back on, looked at her, nodded and grinned. She smiled back and looked ahead. He was something else she didn't want to lose. Men had fooled her before, more times than she cared to remember, but not this one. She had stumbled onto something real and very special this time. Sarah took her hands off the steering wheel and stepped to one side.

"Take us on downriver," Sarah said moving away from the console. Ryan stepped to the controls and pushed the throttle slowly forward, intent on the course ahead. Sarah moved up behind him, wrapped her arms around him and snuggled her chin into his back. "So now you don't quiver and jump when I do this, huh?" she said into the back of his shirt.

"What?"

Sarah snuggled another few seconds, gave a final hug and moved up beside him. "I said you haven't winked at me a single time all day."

"Don't have to. You've been smiling from ear to ear since before breakfast."

Sarah felt herself blushing and her smile widening. "Well, so have you."

Ryan felt Sarah's arm tighten around his waist and glanced down. He couldn't see her face, but he knew there was a smile on it. It felt good to have her next to him, as if she belonged there. It was something she had been telling him all day, even now, that she belonged there, close to him. She said it not in words, but attitude, gestures and... feeling, a sense of ease and connection he had never experienced before, not even with Mary. Mary had never felt she belonged with him. He should have known that. Mary had even told him so, many times, finally in words.

Then Yolanda, the beautiful untamed border canyon enchantress, had literally vanished from his life.

Sarah: strong, smart, loyal and... she loved him. Ryan half-turned from the controls. Leaning over he put his left arm around Sarah and said quietly, "Last night was pretty wild and fantastic...."

"Yes," she agreed and continued, "I especially enjoyed the fantastic part."

He could see the smile on her face now.

Ryan felt his own smile. "Well, today, right now, I want you to know that this moment, this day is... just... wonderful, and there is no place I would rather be." He pulled her tightly against him, leaned over and pressed his lips gently yet firmly against hers.

Yes, wonderful now, wonderful this morning and last night, Sarah thought. Warm snuggly blankets after the icy lake water, this gentle tower of strength and warmth folded against her... just wonderful. She struggled from the spell enough to peek at black-streaked red cliffs drifting by. Leaning the both of them to the right enough, she reached the throttle and pulled it to idle position. She felt Ryan loosen their embrace slightly and look up.

"We're all right," he said softly.

"Yes, we are, and I would like another kiss, just like that one... now, please."

♦ ♦ ♦

The waiting boat was gray and silver, not red, and almost concealed by the billowing white smoke coming from its idling outboard. Ryan moved the Boston Whaler alongside. Fuentes was not on board, but four of his men were; thin-faced Rafael Orosco, George Gomez, the pistol collector, and Fuentes' driver, Miguel Flores.

"He has trouble with the Coast Guard," young Miguel said in reply to Ryan's shouted question about Fuentes. "*El Jefe* ordered them to come. They have found the sailboat and are going to raise it. *El Jefe* is very angry with the Coast Guard captain."

"But he doesn't want to miss the boat rising," Ryan said in a low, disgusted tone as he turned to Sarah. "Let's show them the mine and get the hell out of here."

The four *federales* were armed with large assault-type rifles. They looked surprised when Ryan unveiled Tom's M-1 Garand, loaded it, slung it on his right shoulder and draped three bandoliers of ammunition around his neck. "We had a little trouble here yesterday," he said in Spanish.

Sarah shook her head at the understatement, turned and led the way from the beached boats up to and along the shelf to the corridor. Ryan stepped inside the corridor, flipped over a flat rock and recovered his badge, credentials and pistol he had hidden. He put the credentials and badge into a hip pocket and shoved the pistol into his waistband.

"Up there," he pointed, "beside a large pear cactus is where the man does his shooting. It's hard to see from here. We'll take you over there after you've seen the mine." He looked at Sarah, nodded and motioned with his eyes, as if she should lead the way up the rocky, debris-choked arroyo. Rattlesnake haven. She hesitated. Ryan stepped ahead of her. His leather-soled street shoes slipped on the rubble as he led them to the top of the cliff. He stepped aside, motioning again for her to lead as he stared across the cove. He was making her nervous.

She followed his gaze to the top of the slope on the other side and saw only the haze of blue-green cenizo. She couldn't make out the clump of cactus. The *federales* were waiting. She struck out for the mine, and the men followed. When she glanced back, Ryan had fallen in behind the last man, but was still staring across the cove. She would be glad to get back into the boat and head for the dock.

As they approached the mine, she saw that the heavy iron cover had been pulled aside. "It's open," she shouted, turning to face Ryan.

"Don't do anything stupid," came a voice out of the hole. It was a voice she knew.

She turned back to the mine. Paulson was emerging from the hole, pointing a rifle at her. What was he doing here?

"Drop the rifles," he ordered. He was clear of the hole now, feet spread and expression grim. With his short, white, bristling hair, he had always reminded her of a circus clown. He looked like an evil clown now.

"Craig," she heard Ryan say, "these are Mexican *federales*. They're helping Sarah."

"I don't care who they are. Drop the rifles."

Ryan repeated the order in Spanish. Sarah looked back as Ryan eased his rifle onto the ground by its sling. The Mexicans did the same. She turned back to Paulson. Was he the one? Had he murdered Laura and Mike?

"How long have you been here?" Ryan asked.

"Long enough to see what's here." He nodded toward the opening at his feet, his eyes darting left, right, then back to the six of them, nervous and unsure.

"The opening is wired to a radio transmitter," Ryan said. "Someone is on the way to kill all of us right now."

Paulson narrowed his eyes, surveyed the area again and then turned back to Ryan. When Paulson opened his mouth to speak his head exploded like a ripe watermelon.

Sarah flinched at the sound of the shot, and then froze, staring at the dead man as his body crumpled back into the hole. An arm went around her waist. As she heard a second shot she was carried forward.

"Into the mine, quick," Ryan said.

Another shot rolled across the cove as Ryan deposited her beside the mine opening.

"Inside," he said, dropping to one knee.

She moved to the opening, found the ladder with her left foot, turned and started down. There was the sound of a fifth distant shot as Ryan raised his rifle to his shoulder. She nearly lost her grip on the iron ladder rung as Ryan began firing less than three feet from her face.

◆   ◆   ◆

The sniper brought the rifle back on target. Paulson and one *federale* were down. The crosshairs found another head, this one frozen, staring, like a quail. The rifle bucked, came back aimed at another gawking head, jumped and came down again. This time, the target was in motion. Two quail-shots were the usual limit before the covey flushed. The sniper began the trigger squeeze as he eased the crosshairs ahead of the runner. He had made this shot a thousand times. The *federale* was much slower than a deer or jackrabbit, but just as predictable. The rifle jumped, and the sniper knew the shot was good. He stared through the scope at the sprawled man for an instant then moved on.

He had noticed Shaw and Sarah headed for the mine entrance after the first shot. Dead meat this time. The scope quickly picked them up, Sarah entering the mine, Shaw kneeling on one knee... aiming a rifle? The sniper heard a familiar dull pop as something struck him in the chest. The sound of rifle shots reached him as he sprawled backward. Gravel and rock exploded around him. In the center of the maelstrom, he could only stare up at the cloudless blue sky and try to breathe.

◆   ◆   ◆

Ryan jacked the two remaining rounds and clip from the Garand rifle and reloaded with a full clip. Strange, after all these years he knew exactly how many unfired cartridges remained from the first clip. The six fired rounds had scored three solid hits. His eyes remained glued to the blurred shape beside the large clump of cactus two hundred yards across the cove. There was no movement, but the form lying beside the cactus would have his undivided attention as long as he and Sarah were in the open. "Sarah, are you OK?"

"OK."

"I'm going across the cove. You stay here. I'll wait until you are on the ground below. You still have a flashlight, right?"

"I'm not going down there alone. I'll be right behind you." Ryan decided she was right. He did not want her down there alone either. There was no movement across the cove. He had the rifle. That made him the target. "Stay back away from me until I get to him." Ryan heard her agree as he stepped away from the mine opening. "See if any of these guys are alive." Ryan said as he moved past the first *federale*.

Sarah replied, "OK," which somehow seemed a strange thing for her to be agreeing to. What about Paulson? She glanced down into the darkness as she stepped up off the ladder. He was down there somewhere. She remembered him dropping straight down, instantly, as Ryan rushed her toward the mine. His rifle was still here, at her feet, and empty shell casings from Ryan's rifle. What was Paulson doing here? Why had he threatened them with a rifle? Ryan was twenty yards away, moving slowly toward the end of the cove. Sarah started toward him. The first *federale*, the young one, was on his right side; face-down in a pool of blood. Sarah knew he was dead but knelt and felt for a pulse at his neck. The second officer was the one who had taken her pistol. He was on his stomach, face down, a large bloody hole in the center of his tan shirt. Sarah didn't want to look at or touch him. She moved on slowly past the third one without stopping.

29

"You nailed me dead center, boy," the old man said as Ryan raked the rifle out of the killer's reach with his left foot. Blood soaked the front of the sniper's khaki shirt and streamed into a growing puddle beside him. Ryan stared down into the weathered face. There was not much time. He turned slightly and motioned for Sarah to join him. Turning back to Monte, he asked, "Where did you put the bodies?"

"Pumping pretty good, am I?" The old man stared back into Ryan's eyes. "Can't feel a thing. You nailed me dead center," he repeated, and his attention went to the approaching Sarah. "You were all in it together."

"Where is my sister?" Sarah blurted out as she came up beside Ryan. "Where is she?" Apparently noticing the proximity of her left foot to the puddle of blood, she moved backward a step.

The clatter of tumbling shale from above caused Ryan to also take a step backward, raise the rifle and aim it up the slope toward the sound. A familiar figure emerged from the brush. "Chango," Ryan shouted. "Are you going to shoot at us, too?"

"I'm not armed." Chango continued walking toward them, arms upraised. "You've shot Monte," Chango exclaimed as he arrived and knelt beside the old man.

"See, son, they were all in it together, looking for our mine," Monte said as he glanced toward Sarah and Ryan.

"Yes, yes, you were right," Chango replied softly as he unbuttoned the bloody shirt, shook his head and placed his left thumb on the oozing bullet hole at the base of Monte's sternum. He looked up at Ryan. "Help me get him down to a boat."

"He's bleeding from both sides," Ryan said, "He won't make it to a boat."

"No, I won't make it to a boat," Monte whispered. "Got me dead center, took out my spine... won't make it."

Ryan watched the old man's weathered face relax, all but his eyes that suddenly widened.

"My sister," Sarah shouted. "What about my sister?"

"He can't hear you," Ryan said, quietly.

Chango patted the old man's head and stood up. Turning slowly, he stared first at the rifle in Ryan's hands, then at Ryan.

"Paulson shot him," Ryan lied. The thought had taken shape even as he climbed the slope toward the stricken Monte. It was a story for Mexican officials, now for Chango, too.

"Paulson?" Chango looked surprised.

Probably not as surprised as Sarah, Ryan thought. "He's down there." Ryan nodded toward the cove. "In the mine... dead. Monte shot him... and three *federales*."

"Three *federales*?" Chango looked surprised again.

"Fuentes' men," Ryan said calmly. "And he was going to kill us, too, but of course, you already know that."

Chango inhaled deeply and said, "I told him you were leaving." His attention turned to Sarah. "That he should leave you alone just let you leave."

"Leave me alone?" Now Sarah appeared surprised, but only for a moment. "It was him?" She glanced down at the old man's body. "Monte chased me that day on the lake, tried to break into my... put water in my gas cans... Why?"

"Your sister and her husband uncovered the cave, and Monte killed them just as he has killed others who found the cave. The gold in there played out years ago. When the lake filled, something moved or caved in someplace because of the weight of all the water. We never knew what happened exactly, but the nuggets and gold flakes stopped coming. Maybe it just ran out.... wherever it came from. The water in the cave still flows, but the gold stopped coming. Monte believed it would come back someday."

"So, Monte just killed anyone discovering the cave?" Ryan asked.

Chango nodded, looking away. "He and my grandfather fought with Zapata in the Mexican Revolution. Afterward, Grandfather married into this ranching family here. Monte returned to the United States. He said he robbed trains and banks, got caught, then escaped from prison. He showed up here, long before I was born. Grandfather gave him a job and half the gold he took from the cave. By then, it was not as much as it once had been. Monte took out a few small nuggets and panned some flakes after a heavy rain west of here, but it wasn't much."

"And my sister?" Sarah inquired again.

"She's gone," Chango answered as he turned to face her. "All of them are gone," he continued before Sarah could respond. "The charcoal pits, remember I showed them to you, how some of the fishermen made charcoal to sell by covering the burning mesquite wood? Monte has his own pits like that, back in the hills, but not for making charcoal. He burned all the bodies and took the ashes to the middle of the lake. There is nothing left of any of them... except the mayor and the ones on his boat."

"Monte killed the mayor." Ryan made it a statement rather than a question.

"The college kid," Chango went on. "He opened the cave, set off the signal. Monte said when he got there, he thought everyone he saw was involved, even you, Sarah. He was going to shoot you, too, but you turned around. He said you ruined his shot or something. You were almost killed that day."

Sarah was quiet, staring at the dead man.

"So, everything was a big conspiracy to him." Ryan broke the silence. "The mayor still in his boat at the bottom of the lake?"

"Yes," Chango answered, volunteering nothing further.

"You help Monte with any of his.... executions?

"I tried to stop him. But stories of the lost mine showing up in reports for treasure hunters made him crazy. That's when he rigged up the signal... went really crazy. I helped him with the mayor's boat. We sunk it in the deep water in front of the dam. All the people are inside."

"Fuentes and the Coast Guard are raising it now," Ryan said.

"I know. I wanted the casino people to be blamed. The mayor was fighting them. I don't like them either. They took my land."

"Yes, I've heard about that." Ryan interrupted anything further from Chango on his favorite topic. "Fuentes will be here soon." Slinging Tom's M1 rifle onto his shoulder, Ryan leaned over and picked up Monte's weapon. It was the same as Tom's, old original Army issue but for the scope. He jacked the remaining rounds along with the clip from Monte's rifle into his hand and dropped them into his pocket. The missing clip and unfired rounds would confuse the crime scene, but he would leave that for the Mexicans to sort out. He dropped Monte's now-empty rifle beside the old man.

"Sarah and I are leaving now," Ryan said. "We were never here and we won't be back...ever. Goodbye, Chango." He motioned Sarah down the slope and followed in an awkward half-turned stride, watching Chango. His explanations had come a bit too fast, with a little too much eagerness. Ryan was thinking that when he and Sarah were safely back across the Rio Grande, he wouldn't really care one way or the other about Chango's involvement. He watched Chango move slowly up the slope and disappear into the thick brush. Ryan turned and caught up with Sarah.

♦　　♦　　♦

Sarah watched Ryan kneel at the mine entrance and began retrieving rifle shell casings. He straightened, stared at the casings in his hand and glanced about. "There is one more," he said to himself.

"Some of them hit my hat," she answered. "Maybe it went down the mine..." Then she saw the end of it protruding from beneath Ryan's now thoroughly battered left shoe. Ryan's new street shoes, now gouged and ruined. This was Sarah's first real thought since hearing Chango say Laura and Mike had been... she forced that picture from her mind again. "There it is," she said, pointing to the brass shell under Ryan's foot.

Stepping to the rear, Ryan stooped and plucked the shell from the petrified snail gravel. "Great," he said as he dropped all the shells into his pocket. "I really didn't want to go down there," he nodded toward the mineshaft, "moving Paulson around for it."

"What was he doing here?" Sarah seized on a subject she could tolerate.

"I don't know, Sarah," Ryan replied, staring at the gaping mine shaft. "I don't know much about him, but it seems he was just as crazy as old Monte."

"He was always nice and polite." Sarah could hear herself began to babble. "He fixed up the boat for me, didn't try to overcharge for anything and he finally got a canopy for the Whaler... came in last week." A canopy for the boat – why was she jabbering about a boat canopy she would never use? There were dead people all around her. "I told him to send it back."

"He probably would have killed all of us," Ryan said matter-of-factly as he glanced about again. "To keep his newly-found gold mine a secret. Maybe he overheard one of us tell Fuentes about the mine. Maybe one of those dead *federales* told him."

Ryan leaned over and lifted Paulson's rifle from the ground. "Hold your ears. I'm going to make a little noise now. The Mexican investigators are going to find whatever they are told to find, but just in case they want to wrap things up quickly." Ryan flipped the safety lever off, shouldered the Remington .270 caliber rifle and fired it into the air four times, expelling three empty shell casings. The fourth remained in the rifle. Sarah was puzzled as he removed his T-shirt, until she saw him use it to wipe the rifle clean of fingerprints. He dropped the weapon near the open mineshaft. "Come on, let's get back to the good old U.S.A. and not come back to Mexico for a long, long time."

Ray Summers

30

"For a change, the union wanted nothing to do with the hot potato Banner. He should have listened to his attorney and kept his mouth shut." Internal Affairs Special Agent Fred Ochoa seemed ecstatic. "We've got him. He actually denied even knowing Arispe, lied under oath during the interview. Big-time criminal offense. With the video, the recorded conversation, all the witnesses, and now his own big lying mouth, he's toast, just toast." Ochoa's smile was ear to ear.

"He is all yours, amigo." Ryan said as he finished packing his silver briefcase from the borrowed desk. "You have the whole Customs Service behind you on this one. If you say he's toast, then he's going to be toast." Ryan closed the briefcase and snapped the locks. "Now I have a new Spanish class to get up and running at the training center. It's been my pleasure working with you, Fred." Ryan offered his hand. Ochoa shook it, still grinning.

"That new Spanish class will be starting about three months from now," Ryan said quietly. "And you get a seat on the front row."

◆   ◆   ◆

Ryan drove slowly from the Customs Agents' parking lot toward town. He looked at his watch. He had looked at it often during the long telephone conversation with the commissioner.

Sarah was probably well on her way by now. Someone from a local service station was to meet her at the RV park, prepare the Ranchero to be towed and see that it was hitched behind the motor home. Their farewell had been hurried and awkward; Ryan didn't feel good about it, but there had been the scheduled showdown interview with Banner, then his lengthy report to the commissioner. He looked at his watch again as he topped the railroad overpass. She could be as far as Sanderson by now, depending on how the Ranchero hitching project had gone. Or, she could still be at the RV Park. At the bottom of the overpass Ryan drove straight north instead of making the right hand turn toward San Antonio.

♦ ♦ ♦

He stared at the empty RV space where the Winnebago had been parked. The Boston Whaler had been retired to Mrs. Weaver's backyard last evening. The Ranchero, in all probability trailing behind the motor home, was gone. Most importantly, Sarah was gone. Ryan stared down at the scuffed grass and bare gravel of the empty lot, sorting out zigzag imprints left by Sarah's new blue deck shoes in the sparse patches of dust and sand. This was now a sad lonely place. He wondered if she had stopped for gas before hitting the road.

"She left exactly an hour and a half ago, said she was gassing up in Dryden." A gruff feminine voice answered his thought.

Ryan turned to face Mrs. Weaver, who had quietly walked up behind him. "Hour and a half," Ryan repeated as his thoughts flashed back to another time, a time he had acted too late. A whole year he had waited to follow his Mary overseas.... only to find that she was married.

♦ ♦ ♦

Sarah was trying not to think about Ryan. It was a losing battle. She disliked the way they had been forced to part that morning. No, she admitted to herself, not the way they had parted... just that they had parted. Damn the IRS! There was no way out of the Sunday meeting tomorrow with her attorney. The IRS would be denied no longer. She would be at the formal hearing in Albuquerque on Monday morning or she wouldn't have to concern herself with the gift shop any longer. It would belong to Uncle Sam. Damn! She didn't want to think about any of that, either. Thoughts of Ryan were much more pleasant... even if they hurt.

This was his opportunity to bow out, she was thinking. Perhaps it was for the best that circumstances had given him such a choice. He had promised to come to Socorro as soon as possible. Of course, he was under no obligation to do any such thing, but she was hoping, wanting him to. Was she doing one of the silly coy things men are always saying women do? No, definitely not. She had told him she wanted to see him again. "Hey," she had said, "I know about this cabin in the Sandia Mountains overlooking Albuquerque, horseback access only. Come see me."

The thought of them in the cabin warmed her. Oh, he knew all right, he knew she wanted him. And that she certainly did. With him what you saw was what you got. Not a phony bone in his body. His every thought and action seemed always for her comfort and safety. God, his mind worked fast, the right solution every time. And that night in the boat, if she lived to be a hundred, the image of him in the bow of the boat, silhouetted by the muzzle flashes of his rifle, her behind the wheel of the speeding boat, running down the murderer... those images would never leave her. The two of them were magnificent. Would there ever be another day like yesterday? She rubbed away the goosebumps on her arms. What could possibly be done for an encore to that?

The whoop of a siren outside her window made her jump. She glanced over at the white police car beside her, red and blue lights blinking. She took a quick look at the speedometer: only sixty-five. How long had the policeman been behind her? The patrol car pulled ahead, into the lane in front of her. An arm from the driver's window signaled her to follow. Sarah was puzzled. She followed the police car, noticing the Sanderson, Texas, city-limits sign whiz by on her right.

The patrol car proceeded through the thinly populated outskirts of the small city to the main crossroads of downtown. The white patrol car pulled into a vacant lot across from the S&S Cook Shack restaurant. As Sarah pulled up beside the patrol car, she saw it was marked "Terrell County Sheriff's Office." A tall, thin man in khaki trousers and white long-sleeved shirt exited the sheriff's car. He settled a large-brimmed straw hat onto his head as he approached. Sarah lowered her window and cut the engine. She felt a smile began to slowly creep across her face. No, she had no idea what encore could possibly challenge the happenings of the boat-ramming gun-fight night, but she was pretty sure there was going to be one.

"You are Miss Sarah, aren't you?" the officer asked as he removed his just-settled hat.

"Yes, I am."

"Well, Miss Sarah, my name is Bill Shockley. I'm the sheriff of this county and there is a U.S. Customs agent in Del Rio who has asked me...."

"Sheriff Shockley, does that café across the street serve coffee and pie?"

"Well, yes, ma'am, it sure does." Shockley was smiling. "Just about the best there is."

"Come on, Sheriff. Let's have some pie and coffee while we wait for that Customs agent."

About The Author

 **Ray Summers** knows the United States/Mexico border and its landscapes, culture, people, issues, wonders and merits almost as well as the back of his hand. For 30 years he served in Texas, Arizona and New Mexico as a Border Patrol, Customs and Drug Enforcement Agency agent. His service and his storytelling savvy imbues his modern Western crime sagas with a resonant realness that brings depth and impact to these fictional mysteries/adventures set in the Southwestern borderlands.

A native of the Lone Star State raised in the West Texas town of Monahans, Summers grew up often on horseback, working on ranches and wandering the area's vast wind-blown sandhills, exploring and collecting Native American arrowheads and other artifacts uncovered by the shifting sands. After graduating from high school in 1955, he briefly worked as a lineman for the local power company before attending trade school in Fort Worth and then signing on as a telegrapher and later station agent for the Santa Fe Railroad. Summers also served four years in the Air Force as a mechanic, crew chief and flight engineer on RB66 twin-engine jet bombers.

Ray began his federal law-enforcement career in 1960 with the Border Patrol and then as a special agent with the Customs Service, the newly formed Drug Enforcement Administration in 1973, and then the Customs Internal Affairs unit. During his decades as a criminal investigator, he served in Nogales, Arizona, and such Texas locales as Sonora, Del Rio, Houston, El Paso and Austin, and worked on extended details in New Jersey and New York plus temporary emergency sky-marshal duties mandated by President Nixon in 1970.

On his retirement from federal service in 1990, Summers became a private investigator conducting fraud, theft and arson investigations for various clients and private insurance companies. He married his high school sweetheart, Janet Wynona Cloninger, in August 1956. They have three children, Susan, Alan and Cathy, as well as one grandson, Zachary Shipp, and reside in San Angelo, Texas.

Ray Summers